The Rabbit Princess: The Path

R. CHEN

Cover Art by Ed Chen

Book Art by R. Chen

Text © 2018 by R. Chen

Cover illustration by Ed Chen © 2018.

Interior illustrations by R. Chen © 2018.

All rights reserved. Published 2019 by Osani Studios Inc.

Chen, R., 1975— author.

The Rabbit Princess: The Path / R. Chen

ISBN-13: 978-1-7327189-0-6 (paperback)
ISBN-13: 978-1-7327189-2-0 (e-book)
ISBN-10: 1-7327189-1-3

DEDICATION

For Zoe, Dylan & Judy.

CONTENTS

Hush Osani. Hurry. Over here. Go! Go! Go! Yes, under the roots. Shhhhh. We're safe now. Blue's army won't find us. This burrow will grow hot, but the fire won't reach down here. We'll be safe. I'm too old for this. I'm much too old. Calm down. No, I'm talking to myself. I don't have much more time. Come here next to me. Pull your tail in. Let me hug you.

I feel your heart trembling. Don't be afraid. Tuck those big ears in. There will be an answer. You will see. I was about your age when the war last came. What? Yes, I can tell the story. But this time, I want to tell you a bit more. You have to listen carefully. It'll be important. I don't know how much longer I'll live. Don't be sad. I'm old. I've had a good life. I'm at peace with it. Rest now and listen.

In the middle of Harmony Meadow, on a small peak, an ivory and ruby-trimmed palace soars above the tree-lined horizon with its walls stretching down the rocks into the valley like giant tiger paws clasping onto a prey. When you see this human palace, you will know this is the one I've been telling you about. This is the palace you must find one day. This is where the story starts. The story doesn't start here in Cloud Mountain, nor in Snow Forest. All stories start somewhere and at some time. You just never know where or when. You only know when it's over.

As you walk through the main gate, you'll be mesmerized by the beauty of the palace reflected in a large turquoise pond. Around this pond, olive-colored hedges stand five cranes tall, forming a giant maze that only a few know how to navigate. You'll be greeted by silence— you'll only hear the sound of the wind leaping from leaf to leaf. You may find yourself surprised that no birds, no squirrels, and no other animals play in this garden.

Make your way through this maze—sometimes the path will end, and you'll need to retrace your steps. So, remember your steps and which paths you've gone down. You'll learn. And eventually you'll find your way to the palace walls where a strip of ruby paint runs across the top of the walls and gold etchings glimmer in the evening sun. Examine them carefully. Fighting tigers, pandas, dholes, cranes and monkeys tell a story. Look over the drawings from left to right, and as you near the center of the wall, you'll see an odd-looking, skinny rabbit with a crown. She stands on a log holding a sword in the air. That is the Rabbit Princess.

You're young, and you're naive. So was she. But now, she's a legend we all speak about. Your friends say she's not real. They don't believe the stories. They say I'm old and crazy. Don't shake your head. I know what they say. Growing old is like feeling a single drop of rain—you look up wondering where it came from and whether there'll be more, and soon you even forget what it felt like. It leaves you confused.

I'm rambling now. The Rabbit Princess was real. She freed us. I'm not crazy. I was there. She was my friend. Even if you don't believe me, what matters is that we are inspired. We aspire to be like her. She once was like you. Life is a maze—all who remember and learn, no matter how many twists and turns, eventually find their destiny.

This war is far from over. Snow Forest is burning down as we speak. I won't see the end of it. We're all we have. The only gift I can leave you is this story. One morning, I won't wake. I want you to remember this story and to find this palace. You'll find our friends. You'll discover the truth.

Promise me, Osani. Promise me. That's my good granddaughter.

1. BLOOD

In this palace I've told you about, the Emperor and his family lives, along with his army and his staff of cooks, maids, and other people.

The Emperor, also known as The Heavenly Son of the Forever God of All Eternity, is widowed and has two children, a twelve-year old daughter and a ten-year old son, who is the Crown Prince. In the human world, the Crown Prince is the boy who has the birthright to become the next emperor. The Princess and the Prince torment the staff all day long.

You may wonder why three people live in such a large house. When humans gain more in life, they grow more guarded and protective. They deceive themselves. When you have nothing, the world is open and free—you have nothing to gain and nothing to lose. You aren't afraid. Osani, you and I have nothing except each other. That's why we can freely run from hole to hole each and every night escaping this madness. If we had stuff we cared about, it'd be hard. It'd be very hard to let go.

As I said, in this palace, the Emperor's staff lives. One of them is the chef. She doesn't look like a chef. Her raven black hair drapes around her apple-shaped face and flows down her neck and shoulders. Her long, slender fingers look soft and silky. She's tall and skinny, and looks like she never eats. She appears delicate and beautiful, but she's tough, and she loves food. People thought the Emperor just fell in love with her, and that was the reason he made her the palace chef. When she started, she cooked a feast for the kingdom to celebrate the Emperor's birthday. Once they tasted her food, they knew he was right—she had a special talent.

This chef is miserable because she has to cook the same food every day for his two spoiled children—it's a waste of her talent. The Princess eats dragonfruit sponge cake for every meal, and the Crown Prince wants peanut crusted chocolate mangoes.

One morning, the cook races down to the village to buy some eggs and dragonfruit. She can't find the farmer and asks the fishmonger where he is.

"I don't know," he replies. "I haven't seen him. He may be sick."

"Oh no! This can't be! The Princess will have my head if I don't bake her a cake."

The chef, trying to be clever, finds a lot of other ingredients. Instead of eggs, she buys bananas and apples. She slowly walks back to the palace. She's nervous. Her hands shake, and her basket bounces up and down.

In the palace, she makes her way through a narrow corridor and up the stairs. She trudges into the kitchen which has ceilings stretching four or five elephants high. She yells at the staff to get out. After grabbing all the pots and mixing spoons, she starts to mix up the cake batter. Then, she pulls a cage out of the top cabinet. A little lime green lizard pokes its head out between the bars. Its two large eyes pop wide open, and its long, thin, pink tongue darts in and out. The chef pulls the lizard out of the cage. She tickles the lizard's feet. It laughs so hard it pees into the cake batter. She puts the lizard back in the cage, finishes mixing and puts the cake in the oven.

Later that morning, the stressed-out chef hears the Princess' heels stomping down the hall. She wipes down her apron, brushing off the flour and spices. She blows the hair out of her face. She turns around. Splat!

The chef stumbles backwards, slips on frosting on the floor, and crashes down on the gray and white kitchen tiles. She wipes the cake off her face. She grabs her butt which stings from the fall. A malicious laugh echoes through the room. "Ha! Did everyone see that?" snarls the Princess, dressed in a red and gold trimmed silk shirt and pants. She throws her long black hair back over her shoulders. Her shirt has the Emperor's emblem sewn on the back with gold trims—a dragon wrapped around the sun. "That's what happens when you disappoint me!"

"Your Highness, the Forever Beauty Who Shines Brighter Than the Sun! What did I do? Whatever I did to injure you was never intentional," begs the chef. She scrambles to her knees and crawls across the kitchen to the door where the Princess stood. Falling at the Princess' feet, the chef kisses her black felt shoes.

"Ewww! Get away from me. You're covered in cake. You should be clean when talking to a princess. You're so disgusting!" screams the Princess whose black hair flowed around her oval face and down her neck and back. Her thin eyebrows furrow as her dark eyes glare at the chef. She crumples her small nose and purses her lips in repugnance. She kicks the chef in the chin. The chef falls down in tears, clutching her chin with her hands. Her chin is cut and bleeding. The other cooks run in to help.

The Princess backs away and says, "This cake is disgusting, just like you. How dare you try to fool me! How dare you expect me to eat something so tasteless! A cake...a cake should melt in your mouth like butter, and it should be ever so sweet like ice cream. This! This tastes like day-old bread used to make croutons for your dinner salad. Just like all your ideas—they're old!"

"I'm so sorry, my Princess, the Forever Beauty Who Shines Brighter Than the Sun. It'll be better next time. I'll make another one now. I'll make sure it's moist and sweet," pleads the chef. She stays knelt at the Princess' feet.

The Princess bends down and lifts the chef's chin with her index finger. She whispers, "You needn't worry because there will be no next time. Guards! Take her away! Throw her in the dungeon to think about her crime. Find me another chef!"

The Princess sweeps her finger across the chef's back, wiping the blood off. The chef cries and begs for mercy as two guardsmen carry her kicking and screaming away. Everyone hears her wails through the corridors of the palace. Soon, the hysterical howls turn into sobs, and shortly thereafter, the palace is silent.

2. A USELESS LIFE

Slam! The door bangs against the wall as her brother, the Crown Prince, throws it open. In his navy blue silk shirt and pants, he storms barefoot into the Princess' room. "What did you do?!" he yells. "I'm starving, and you got rid of our cook! She hadn't made my breakfast yet!"

"She screwed up my cake. I had no choice, but to..."

"To what? To ruin my day? It's always about you. You, you, you!"

"Oh, shut up!"

"You shut up!" he yells, and he throws a pillow at her face. Although two years younger, he stands almost as tall as the Princess. He has a strong, thick body—you can tell he'll grow up big and strong. His box-shaped face with his thick eyebrows, long eyes and wide mouth is like his father's. Next to him, the Princess looks much smaller than she really is. She's lean, but she's quite athletic, having studied kung fu, gymnastics and horse riding all her life.

"You ungrateful brother. You don't know how good you have it. You don't know how hard it is to be me. I have to make sure everyone here is working and performing to their best. She tried to trick me with filth. She would've done the same to you, and you, you wouldn't even notice."

"Whatever, you're so pretentious. You think it's all about you." He slams the door shut, and she hears his footsteps echo through the hall.

She sighs and mumbles, "Useless. Everyone's so useless."

The Princess looks up at the ceiling and pulls a cord next to her bed. The ceiling curls and rolls itself up, revealing a light azure sky with scattered white clouds. She takes a deep breath. She stands up and looks out the window. Her big eyes follow the long white palace walls down to the village, where the walls surround the villagers like a prison. She wonders how they all live with themselves, being so useless and all. "I'd kill myself if I was so useless," she whispers to herself. Gazing out into the distant mountains, she wonders what is out there. Her father came from one of those mountains, but she's not sure which one. She also knows there are terrible people out there as well as animals. Her father defeated them all to unify the kingdom and to bring peace. If anyone got a hold of her or her brother, they'd be able to break the peace. She's that important she reminds herself.

The Princess pulls the cord to close up the ceiling, leaves her room and wanders the hallway. A few doors down, she enters the music chamber and sits on the piano bench. A piano is this beautiful musical instrument, Osani. Made out of wood, it stretches wide and deep. Its painted black. A human sits down on a bench and places her hands on small white and black wooden blocks. When she moves her fingers across these boards, beautiful tenor and bass sounds come out of the instrument. It has foot pedals that stretch its sound. Oh, how I wish we had one.

As the Princess sits down, she yells, "Piano player! Come and play the piano!"

A tall, lanky young man with disheveled hair runs into the room, straightens out his black silk clothes and sits himself next to her. He runs his hands through his hair, combing and cleaning it out. He says, "What would you like to hear, my Princess, the Forever Beauty Who Shines Brighter Than the Sun?"

She answers, "I'm bored. I want some music."

He plays a classical piece. She yawns and says, "I've heard that one. Try something more fun."

"What would you like to hear?" he asks nervously.

She throws a book at his head. He ducks. She screeches, "I don't know! That's your job! Figure it out!"

The pianist turns around and starts playing a fast-paced dance song. He sings along. She dances around the room, humming the melody. She can't remember the words and gets frustrated. From across the room, another book comes hurtling towards him and hits him hard in between the shoulder blades. "Owww!" he howls as he falls off the bench, collapsing on the ground.

The Princess walks over and kicks him several times in the lower back. She leans down and says, "Get out of here, you worthless musician. Hurry out of here before I throw you in jail!"

The pianist scrambles to his feet and races out of the room. Now these stories may sound extreme, but they are true. The Princess told me herself. We spent many nights in carefree spirits as well as hiding from harrowing horrors. I learned much about her youth and much about humans. These are the reasons why I often am grateful to be a jerboa. My big ears and long tail aren't much to complain about—they are blessings in disguise.

After the pianist runs out, the Princess sighs. She walks over to the window, overlooking the large front lawn. While braiding her long, coal black hair, she sighs at the sight of her head-shaven brother running across the lawn with a stick.

In his navy blue silk short-sleeve shirt and pants, the Prince runs behind a hedge, looks around and darts across the lawn to another hedge. He lifts the stick over his head as if it's a sword. Pretending to fight an army and chasing down imaginary people, he works himself into a sweat. He jumps and rolls. He pops up and stabs enemies. He yanks his stick out like a sword. He screams victory. All the groundskeepers turn around to see the commotion before turning back to their work.

Falling to the ground, tired and exhausted, he waves his hand in the air. The butler runs out with a glass of iced tea. The boy drinks it all. The butler runs back and gets another glass. The Prince sits up and finishes the second glass. He stares up at the summer sun. He wipes the beads of sweat from his brow. He walks over to a grove of trees, pulls down his pants and pees.

3. PRIDE & JOY

Later that afternoon, the Princess and the Crown Prince are walking towards the courtyard when they spot some of the staff gathered around the Emperor's statue. One of them spies them, and they disband. The Princess demands, "What are you all doing? What are you talking about?"

The head maid replies, "Nothing, your Princess, the Forever Beauty Who Shines Brighter Than the Sun. We're planning out the day."

"I don't believe you. What are you talking about?"

"I'm not lying. We're planning today's schedule. We do this everyday. Usually, we meet in the kitchen, but .... Today, we decided to meet outside because ... the weather is nice."

The Princess stares into the maid's eyes and replies, "Fine. Be on your way."

The maid kowtows and says, "Thank you, your Princess, the Forever Beauty Who Shines Brighter Than the Sun."

The staff all leave the courtyard. The Princess whispers to her brother, "They're up to something. I don't know what it is, but I'm sure of it."

"You're too suspicious. It'll ruin you."

"You're too naive. It'll ruin you." She punches his shoulder, and he glares at her.

The two of them wander around the courtyard for several minutes. The Crown Prince collapses and sighs, "Uggghhhh, I'm so bored. We do the same thing everyday. Where's father?"

"He's checking the great wall. He's making sure the barrier is set. The rebels are organizing in the east."

"How do you know so much?"

"I listen, not like you."

"Whatever."

"Whatever," she mimics him.

He stands up and glares at her. "I hate you."

"Whatever." She walks over to the statue and continues, "How are you going to be Emperor if you don't pay attention? You don't know anything. I should be the Empress."

"You can't be. I'm the Crown Prince. It's already decreed."

"Blah blah blah. Name the five kingdoms father unified."

"I don't have to."

"Exactly my point. You don't know anything." She pauses and then continues, "Have you been practicing your kung fu?"

"Yes, that's fun."

"Swords?"

"Yes."

"Nunchucks?"

"Yes."

"Bo staff?"

"Yes, yes, yes."

"Good."

"How about you?" asks the Crown Prince.

"Of course, I can still beat you."

"No, you can't."

She approaches him, and they stare at each other. Then she starts to laugh. "You're so silly."

"Let's fight!"

"Alright," she replies. They step away from each other, bow and then set up in ready position.

The Princess leaps to the left and does a sweeping kick. The Prince hops over. The Princess leans into an upper punch trying to hit his chin. The Prince dodges the punch and reaches in to grab the Princess' belt. He yanks her down to the ground, and he lands a soft elbow in the small of her back. She yells and grimaces. She turns over. He stands over her with his fist an inch away from her face. She pushes herself off the ground, wiping the dirt and gravel off her face and clothes.

9

They stand facing one another again. "1-0," says the Princess.

They bow. This time, the Princess waits for the Prince to attack. He doesn't. They stand still for a few minutes. The Princess grows impatient. She half jumps over towards him, trying to fake him out. He doesn't move. She aims a kick at his left ribs, he blocks her right shin, and he flips her over. She lands on her feet and hands. She looks up from her push up position. Sweeping his legs, she revels at her first take down. She flips and tries to land an elbow on his chest. He rolls over in time. Her elbow catches the hard gravel floor. She grimaces in pain. Pressing his hands behind his head, he flips himself up onto his feet. He runs towards her, pulls up and throws his hands in front, punching his sister hard in the chest. She falls backwards and crashes hard against the gravel courtyard floor. All her breath escapes her. She's dizzy. He presses his knuckles against her throat and says, "2-0. I win."

She smiles and says, "I'm proud of you, brother. I'm surprised. You really have been practicing."

He sets down his fists and helps her stand up. "Thanks, I love it."

"I can tell. You're thinking about your next move before you even make your current one."

"I'm actually thinking about my next-next move. Master Tao says I need to see the whole fight in my mind before I even start." He steps back and bows.

The Princess stares at her brother and a smile comes across her face. She is filled with pride and joy for the first time at her brother. She gives him a hug. He doesn't know what to do. He just says, "What are you doing?"

"I really am proud of you."

"Thanks," he replies, and he steps back.

He walks around the courtyard. "Can we go down to the village? I haven't been there in a year…since mother died. I wonder what's going on."

She thinks about it and answers, "I guess so. General Sun is out with father, so I'll ask Master Tao to join us."

4. CHOSEN DESTINIES

With the harsh summer afternoon sun beating down on their faces, the Princess and the Crown Prince head down to the village on their large nutmeg stallions. They are escorted by Master Tao—a short, squatty bald-headed old man—and five guardsmen. The guardsmen have to run along behind them. As they pass the villagers, people approach the dirt road and kowtow. They all chant, "We are not worthy your Princess, the Forever Beauty Who Shines Brighter Than the Sun, and neither are we worthy of you, your Crown Prince, the Honorable and Most Distinguished Sovereign of the Sun."

The village children bring out gifts and food. The Princess ignores them. She even kicks the gifts out of their hands. She says to her brother, "Ugh, I forgot how unworthy they are of us. So useless. So disgusting. Do they actually expect us to eat that stuff or to even touch it?"

Her brother shows some compassion and replies, "I don't know. They don't have much. It's all they can offer."

She stares at him in shock. "What did you say?"

He shrugs his shoulder. "What?"

"I can't believe we're related. We're royalty. They're not. Remember that. How can you be Emperor if you sympathize with them? You have to rule them. They're not worthy of your presence. If we were all equal, what would be of this world? It'd be chaos. How could you live where everyone was treated equally? Who would rule? Who would bring peace and order?"

He tries to answer, but she continues, "Think about it. If you treat a villager as an equal, then they'd all want to be treated the same. If they are equal to you, then why would you be the Emperor? Why would you be the one sent from heaven? There'd be no reason someone else shouldn't be the Emperor. It'd be chaos. Father fought and unified all the kingdoms to bring order and peace. Without him, we'd all be in constant war."

"I suppose you're right," he answers. "But I can't help that there's something we've missed. We're all different. Not everyone would be a ruler. Look at you and me. We're different."

"Stop right there!" The Princess tugs on her reins and halts her horse. Everyone else stops. She points at her brother and says, "We are different. We're the rulers. They are the servants. Get that straight in your head!"

Shading his eyes, the Prince glances down at the villagers but feels saddened by the whole scene. He understands his sister's points, but he believes there must be some other way. It didn't seem right to treat people this way. He looks around at the villagers' faces and remembers his mother. She grew up here before being married to their father. He liked being here. It reminded him of her. He remembers her last day. She asked him where his sister was, he didn't know, and she closed her eyes. His mother said, "Always remember me, and don't grow up to be like your father and sister. We're family, we'll always be together. But you can choose another path, another way of treating people. People are born into their situations. They have no control over that. But we all control our destinies."

As they plod their way back up the hill, they approach a small shop. The shop seemed to be carved out of a large broken tree trunk with roots and branches growing out of the sides. A few openings had been roughly cut out of the sides for windows. A warm orange glow from a fire flickered inside, but there wasn't a chimney. A worn out sign hangs from one of the branches. No one could read the words. "Stop!" yells the Princess. "What is this place? I can't make out that sign."

Master Tao, in his deep, quiet voice, replies, "I believe it's a shaman's shop. We should continue on. No good will come of this."

"No! Why haven't they come out to honor and respect us? Who lives here?"

"I don't know, your Princess. I haven't been here before, but I don't think we should stay. I don't have a good feeling."

She turns around on her horse and glares at him. "Get off your horse and knock on that door!"

Master Tao does as he's told. He dismounts his horse and waddles over to the house on his short, squatty legs. He looks like a walking turtle. An elderly hunched woman opens the door. Her white-gray hair shoots out in every direction making her look like a bent-up, leafless shrub. Her ankles, showing under her paper bag dress, look like twisted tree roots. She grasps onto her dusty black shawl as it keeps slipping. With her other hand, she pushes her glasses back up her crooked nose. Master Tao bows and asks her, "Why aren't you outside kowtowing? Don't you know the royal family is here? Do you have children or grandchildren? Where are their gifts of offering?"

The Princess and the old woman stare at one another. The Princess feels a chill through her body and looks away. She notices the woman's shadow looks like a serpent winding around itself. The woman replies, "I'm sorry. I'm old and don't hear well. Please forgive me. I didn't know they were here."

The old woman steps out the door. As she approaches the Princess, a little boy runs out and yells, "Don't grandma! Don't kowtow! They're horrible!"

The Princess glares at the boy. She looks at the old woman who doesn't reproach the boy. The Crown Prince watches the scene. The Princess orders, "Throw him in jail. I don't like them. They've dishonored us."

The old woman screams, "No!!!! He's my grandson. His parents are dead. He's all I have, and I'm all he has."

She grabs the Princess' leg. The Princess kicks her off, leans down, shoves the old woman in the face, and says, "I don't really care. You two disgust me, and you two should be put out of your miseries."

The old woman falls down, crying and reaching out for her grandson. His hands stretch out as he kicks and screams for her. The entire village witnesses the scene. The Crown Prince and Master Tao are uncomfortable. The Crown Prince feels nauseous and disgusted at his sister. Master Tao whispers to the Princess, "We should return to the palace. We're causing a scene, and we don't have enough men to protect you and the Prince."

The group of them gallop back up the hill to the palace. The guardsmen take the boy and throw him in the dungeon. They take some compassion on him and put him in the same cell as the cook. She hugs him and wipes away his tears. She tells him everything will be alright. He stops crying and whispers, "I know."

5. LESSONS TO BE LEARNED

In the early evening, the Emperor, the General and the army return from their search. The broad and tall Emperor, still dressed in his silver and iron armor, receives word that his children went down to the village and a mild commotion was stirred. He's tired and exhausted from the excursion. He's grouchy and yells, "Annie! Pika! Get down here!"

The Princess and the Crown Prince race through the halls down to the courtyard. They bow their heads, and they don't dare look up. He paces in front of them, and then stops. He leans over the Princess' head and growls, "What were you thinking? I told you to never leave the palace without me or General Sun. How dare you?!"

"I'm sorry Father. I wasn't thinking," she whimpers. She looks up at her father's dirt covered black bearded face. The wrinkles have deepened on his forehead and around his eyes. His cheeks seem more chiseled on his box-shaped face.

"That's right. And now, the villagers are upset. They say you threw a young boy into jail. Whatever for?"

"He didn't kowtow, and he mocked us."

The Emperor leans down and lifts up her chin. "Really? That's why? How will you children ever learn to rule? That's the stupidest reason I've ever heard. For that, you've ruined our reputation and legacy. That's all we have!"

The Crown Prince doesn't say a word. He wipes his nose as he sniffles and quietly cries. The Emperor leans towards him and says,

15

"And what about you? What did you do?"

"Nothing. Sister got mad and ordered the boy to be taken."

"And you just watched?"

"Yes."

"You are the Crown Prince. You have final word. You didn't do anything. The people saw that. You'll have to earn their respect now." He pauses and stands up, casting his shadow over them. "Children, have you learned nothing? I am Emperor because I battled and fought my way to victory. People follow me because I led us to victory and peace. I put my life on the line for them. People follow me because they respect me…even if it's out of fear. But you two…you two have nothing. They can't fear you. You haven't accomplished anything. They'll overthrow you, just like that. The army won't follow you. They follow me because we've shed blood side by side. I've held their dying brothers and fathers in my arms. But your treacheries erase all memories of what I've done. Look at history, and you'll see this lesson."

"Yes, father," both children answer.

"Now, get dressed for dinner. Tomorrow, I'll deal with this nonsense," the Emperor orders. He stomps out of the courtyard with the sound of clanging armor trailing him.

The children meander back to their rooms. In the hallway, the Crown Prince says, "It's all your fault. I told you not to throw the boy in jail. And then you had to act so important and all. He was just a boy."

"Whatever, you act so righteous now. You didn't say anything then. Father said you have final word. You didn't do anything, but you could have."

"That's because you never listen."

"If you can't order me—your sister—around, then how are you going to lead a country?" she asks and stares at him.

The Prince doesn't reply. He just walks on to his room. The Princess looks on and walks back to her room. She mutters to herself, "Useless. He'll fail as Emperor. Father's right. He's weak."

She slams her door and throws herself on the bed. She knows she's right about the boy. He'd never learn his lesson unless he was in jail. She did the right thing. People need to be taught a lesson and put in their place. If they don't, then chaos would ensue. She tells herself that her father was just trying to teach her brother a lesson. She turns over and looks up at the ceiling. She stands up and looks out the window. The sun is setting over the mountains in the distance, and the shadows cast from the palace are falling over the village. Some of the lights are turning on. She likes this time of the day. She changes into her yellow and red evening gown and walks downstairs.

6. RISE & FALL

Dinner is quiet. Clean and dressed in black and gold-stitched silk, the Emperor sits at one end, eating quietly. He hasn't had a real meal in several days. The food tastes different, but he doesn't dwell on it. He enjoys each bite and drinks some wine. The Princess sits on his left side, and the Crown Prince is on his right. They quietly turn their food over and occasionally take a bite. Both of them aren't hungry. The Prince is saddened by the Emperor's lecture; the Princess is mad and frustrated. They don't know what to talk about. The silence drives the Emperor crazy.

"Someone, please start talking," the Emperor says. "I'm gone for four days, and I come back to this—this silence. What kind of children are you? What have you been doing?"

The Crown Prince replies, "You know what we did. We got into trouble."

"That was a long time ago. I've forgotten it. What did you do today? Other than getting into trouble."

The children remain quiet. The Emperor lets out a heavy sigh and goes back to eating.

The door slams open, and the portly black-bearded General Sun rushes in with his clanging armor and weapons. "Forgive me, my Emperor. The villagers are protesting. They want the boy freed. They're marching up the hill. I've ordered the army to stand them down. You should come speak to them."

The Emperor slams his chopsticks and glass down. He glares at the Princess and says, "See what you've done."

She nervously looks away. The Crown Prince doesn't look up. The Emperor stands up. "General, make sure my children are safe. Take them to the secret chamber."

"Yes, my Emperor."

The Emperor walks out. General Sun, in his black military dress, steel armor and sheathed sword, approaches the children and says, "Come with me. We have no time to lose. The villagers are restless, and you should be in safe hiding."

The Crown Prince stands up and hurries over. The Princess remains seated.

The General says, "Princess! We must hurry."

She replies, "Whatever, we live in a palace. What can they do to us? They can't get in. The army will protect us. The Emperor will take care of this. We should sit and enjoy our meal."

The General walks over and grabs her by the armpit. He lifts her up. She screams in pain. He ignores her and drags her towards the door. She yells, "Let me go! I'll tell the Emperor."

"Go ahead. He told me to take care of you. If you're so stupid that you don't know what is happening, then Heaven protect us all."

"What do you mean? What's happening?" asks the Crown Prince. He follows them out the door.

"The villagers have had enough. They're revolting. The army is just an extension of the village—the army is made up of villagers and others. As soon as they see their friends and family coming, they won't hurt them. As soon as they heard what happened to the boy, they'll question us. The Emperor has to calm this storm you two created. If he doesn't, we'll be in trouble."

"What did you do?!" yells the Crown Prince as he stares at the Princess. "What's wrong with you? Why can't you be a good person?"

"Whatever, I'm not worried," she replies. She brushes the General off and walks on her own.

General Sun pulls his hand back to hit her but quickly stops himself. He remembers his promise to the Empress, not to the Emperor. General Sun was the one who found the Empress in the courtyard well. She had thrown herself in to escape her depression and hallucination. He pulled her out and carried her back to her room. He dried her and dressed her. He laid her on her bed and gently brushed her hair. As she awoke, she smiled at him and said, "General Sun, I always believed you would find me. I know how you feel about me. I can't do this anymore. He's cruel. He's ruthless. He's obsessed with adding to his kingdom and killing those who stand in his way. Annie is like him. I love her, but I don't know her. It may be too late. Pika…Pika is good but will be corrupted. My soul can't bear watching their destinies be ruthlessly taken. I've lost all hope. Promise me you'll protect Annie and Pika."

General Sun grabs both children's hands and pulls them down the hall. They approach the Emperor's room. The Crown Prince says, "We can't go in there. That's the Emperor's room."

"We have to go in. The secret chamber is in there."

The Princess replies, "We don't need to go in there. We're safe here."

The General stops and grabs the Princess by the shoulders. He yells, "What's wrong with you? Don't you understand we're not safe? You may not see your Father again. You and your brother may be killed tonight. The people hate you. No one likes you. I'm the only one who is going to protect you tonight. Anyone else in this palace will kill you when they get the chance. Are you so spoiled that you don't see this?"

The Princess wrenches herself away and runs back down the hall towards her room. The Crown Prince doesn't know what to do. He believes the General but wants to stay with his sister. The General says, "Let her go. Come on."

The Crown Prince changes his mind and screams, "I have to get her! She's my sister! It's stupid, but she's all I have. I lost my mother. I may lose my father. I can't lose her."

The Crown Prince runs down the hall. The General chases after them. He catches up to the Crown Prince, grabs him and carries him along. They burst into the Princess' room. "Where are you?" yells the General. He sets the Prince down. They look all around. The Prince opens up the Princess' armoire and says, "Not here." He shuts it. The General looks under the bed and reaches with his hand. He yanks the Princess out.

The General says, "Do you really think they wouldn't look under the bed?"

"Yes. Why would they? If they got in, they'd just want clothes and stuff."

"You really are a piece of work. You really have no clue, do you?"

20

"Shut up!" yells the Princess.

The General pulls them back down the hall towards the Emperor's room. It's too late. A group of villagers with swords and clubs approaches them. They turn around, and another group surrounds them. The Princess finally realizes the trouble they're in. She holds on tight to the General. The Prince does too. The General pushes them back into the Princess' room. He blocks the door with the armoire and other furniture. The villagers pound on the door. The furniture barricade shakes and shudders. He looks out the window. He says, "They are going to kill me. For you two to survive, you have to be quiet and just agree to whatever horrible words they say about you and the Emperor. You have to go with it. If you fight, they will surely kill you."

He turns to the Crown Prince and says, "You have to live to fight another day. Do you understand?"

The Crown Prince nods. The General adds, "Remember your mother. Remember the good in her."

The armoire and furniture topple over as the door breaks open. Dozens of villagers storm into the room. They grab the General and separate him from the children. The Princess and Crown Prince yell, "No, keep him with us. Please!".

The villagers ignore them. A few of them take the General away. The Crown Prince remembers the General walking out with his head high with dignity and a brave smile across his face.

The Princess and the Prince are tied up and thrown onto the bed. A man in his late 40s with scraggly gray-black hair walks up to them. He turns their heads to get a good look. He scratches his unshaven chin. He smiles, turns around and screams with joy to the villagers. The other villagers rejoice. He looks back at the children and says, "You two forgot to kowtow. Oh, wait. You don't want to? Then off to jail!" He laughs and then continues, "How do you two like it now? You treat us worse than dirt, and now you shall feel retribution."

He faces the villagers and commands, "Put them in the dungeon. We'll wait for Shaman Wu. She'll decide their fate."

7. CLARITY

"Where's father?" whispers the Prince. The dungeon cell is dark, cold and damp. It smells like moldy cheese. The walls are made of uneven boulders that jab and cut into you if you lean against them. The bars on the door look and feel like steel bones. Ants and beetles crawl across the gravel and sand ground. Only a flickering candle down the hall provides any light. The Prince barely makes out his sister's face. It's the first time he's seen her sad and defeated. He sits close to her because he is scared.

"I don't know," she says while wiping away tears. She looks up at the wall. She then grows angry. She stands up. "How dare they do this to us! Don't they know who we are?"

"I think that's the problem."

"Wait!" exclaims the Princess. She grabs the Prince and is excited. She squeezes her face into the space between the bars on her jail cell door. Her eyes are wide open, and she looks this way and that way. "Cook! Boy! Answer me! This is the Princess!"

"What are you doing?"

She sits next to her brother and answers, "Don't you remember all the people I ordered to be jailed. They must be down here somewhere. They'll help us get out."

"Why would they? You put them here."

"Yes, because I'm their Princess. If I wasn't their Princess, I wouldn't be able to order them to be jailed. They still have to obey me."

The Prince stares at his sister in disbelief. He shakes his head and says, "Don't you get it? You put people here for no good reason! They hate you! That's why we're here! They're going to kill us."

She stares back at him in defiance. She still believes she can get out by commanding someone. Grabbing the bars, she yells, "Who's there? Come here! I order you."

Several minutes pass before laughter is heard. A couple of young boys ramble their way down the corridor. The lantern they carry flickers and bounces light from the wall to the ceiling to the floor. They are telling jokes and laughing. They are bragging about their triumphs. As they approach, the Princess reaches out her hand and says, "Come here! I need to get out!"

The skinny disheveled boys walk up to the door and jest, "Oh sure, we'll let you out. No problem."

They laugh. The short, big nosed one says, "Just a minute. I have to find the keys." He pretends to fumble in his pockets for some. The Princess realizes he only has one arm.

She asks, "What happened to your arm? If you want it back, free us, and I'll get you one."

The mood changes. The boys are suddenly silent. The short one looks at the tall one. He then looks at the Princess and replies sarcastically, "What happened to my arm? What happened to my arm?!" He pauses and then continues, "Well, dear Princess, don't you remember?"

"No. But whatever it was, I will have that person thrown in jail, and I'll ask the doctors to fix your arm."

"That person is already in jail. And no doctor can fix my arm. It's gone. And it's gone because that person is you, you wretched devil!"

The Princess steps back aghast. The Crown Prince is shocked. The short boy leans in and says, "Three years ago, you came through the village. There was a drought. My father couldn't farm enough. All we could offer was some vegetables. You kicked our basket over and demanded oranges. We didn't have any. You commanded the guards to throw me in jail and cut off my useful hand."

The Prince sits down on his blanket and doesn't know what to say. The short boy glares at the Princess and lets the silence grow. He spits at both of their feet. "Your deaths can't come soon enough. Come on, let's go." He grabs the lantern, and the two boys walk off. They soon start laughing again.

When the cell grows dark again, the Crown Prince mumbles, "I hope you're happy."

"Shut up!"

"What now?"

"I'm thinking. Obviously, these people don't understand how things work."

"Really? You still believe that?"

"Yes."

"I can't believe you," he says. Standing up, he brushes off his pants and walks to the door. He looks out the cell. He realizes all the other prisoners have been released and wonders where they're keeping his father. He must be somewhere. Then the Crown Prince comes to a realization. He turns to his sister and asks, "Where's father? We're the only ones down here. Where are they keeping him and the General? If they're not here, then they must be dead."

The Prince falls to his knees, crying and shaking. The Princess is caught off-guard. She never thought about it—he may be right. Where would they be? Wouldn't they be here in the jail cells? Where's the rest of the army? Could they have escaped? Would they be dead? No! Her father was great. He couldn't be killed. He would've escaped. He'll be back for them. All these questions start to rush through her mind. She breathes hard and fast. Her heart is beating fast. She hyperventilates. The Prince grabs her and hugs her.

"Calm down," he says. "It'll be alright. I'm sure they're fine."

She grabs him tight. All the crazy thoughts racing through her mind, her thumping and stabbing heart, and her trembling and shaking hands grow into a moment of pure clarity—she just wants her family safe.

8. TRIAL

SLAM!!

"Ow! My eyes!" cries the Prince. All the lanterns are lit. The Prince's eyes try to adjust, but only blinding white light pierces through his mind. His eyes soon start to make out the gray stones in the cell. On the wall, he spots an etching of a three-eyed horny dragon monster eating a bunch of stick figures. He looks down at the dirt on his hands and his black nails. Sitting up on his blanket, he glances across at his sister. She isn't her beautiful self. She's pale and squalid. She's dirty and her torn gown hangs limp off her. Her hair is drained of any fullness and richness—it sags and droops across her back.

"Wake up!" yells an older portly man with a toothless mouth and a lazy eye. He bangs the rusty iron bars with his sword. The clanging metal racket reverberates down the stone corridor. Several other men stand around yelling and making noises. They all want to see the two royal children.

The Princess slowly sits up. She's lost track of time. She doesn't know how many days have passed, or if it's only been many hours. She no longer counts meals to track the passage of time. She's resigned herself to never getting out. She squints and tries to get past the blinding light. She sees the group of men and whispers to herself, "This must be it. It's time to die."

The men enter the cell and grab the two children. The men push the children down and shackle their hands and feet with heavy, iron chains and cuffs. The children are led down the old corridor. They shuffle and drag their feet as the iron shackles weigh them down. The men walk in silence. The Prince asks questions that no one answers. The Prince and Princess have no energy. What probably is a short walk feels like miles because they are so weak and tired. Both of them just want to die at this point.

The short skinny man in front opens up a door, and sunlight floods the corridor. Both of the children shield their eyes. They haven't seen the sun in what feels like forever. A big burly guardsman knocks both of them down with blows to their necks. The other guards drag the two of them along the stone and gravel path. Cheers and jeers erupt from a large crowd. The children are dragged up stone steps. When they are dropped, the Princess looks up and sees her father. Her eyes open wide, and her mouth drops. He is beaten and bloodied. His beautiful black beard now is crimson, brittle and stained with dried blood. His eyes are swollen. He is hanging by his tied up hands from a beam up high. Next to him, she sees the General. Neither of them can see her and the Prince. They both seem to be unconscious.

"Nooooooo!" screams the Prince. He sees his father and the General. He's first filled with relief that his father is alive after believing he was dead for all these days. Anger rages within the Prince. Blood is pulsing, and he struggles to free himself. He screams, "I'll kill you all!!!"

With his sword's handle, a guard hits the back of the Prince's skull, knocking him out. The Princess winces. She looks longingly at her father, feeling relieved that he's alive. She had cried and mourned for all those days. Then she realizes they're all on a platform above the courtyard. Someone she can't see is talking at the front, and hundreds of villagers are standing in the courtyard, yelling and chanting. The villagers are calling for their deaths.

The person speaking stops. The person turns and approaches the Princess. She can only see the feet. It's a woman? The Princess sees red slippers and exposed ankles. On the slippers, there is an emblem of a serpent wrapped around the moon. She realizes the person is wearing a dress, or at least a skirt. In her twisted position, she can't look up. Suddenly, a guard yanks her hair, snapping her head back. She stares into a familiar but unrecognizable face.

"Hello Princess," whispers the woman. Who is this woman? She bends down to look at the Princess. Her wavy jet black hair flows around her peach-shaped face, and her golden skin radiates with youth

26

and energy. She has a warm smile, but her eyes…her eyes are dark, ebony stones sitting in hearths of pure white snow. Her eyes are almost lifeless and infinitely deep—the Princess is hypnotized by her reflection in them. The woman touches the Princess' cheek with her long, slender index finger. Her long clear nail looks like an eagle's talon and flows like a river from the Princess' high cheek along the edge of her mouth down to her chin, dropping off like a waterfall. The woman almost reminds the Princess of her mother. The woman stands straight up. The sun casts her shadow long behind her. Seeing this shadow shaped like a serpent snaps the Princess out of her trance, and she realizes who this woman is.

"Are you…"

"Yes, you put my boy in jail. You picked the wrong people to abuse."

The Princess fights to break free but can't. She yells, "I'll kill you!"

"Oh really? Look up. I wanted you and your brother to at least have the opportunity to say goodbye to your father and his general." She points up to them on their posts.

"I'll kill you!"

"Is that really what you want to say to them?" the woman slyly says. "Are those really your last words to your father?"

"Who are you?"

The woman kneels down and leans in. She holds the Princess' chin. "In due time, child. In due time." She straightens out and continues, "Now, let's move on, shall we?"

The woman directs the guards to the Emperor and the General. She faces the crowd and decries, "The people have accused the Emperor and the General of acts against humanity—they have murdered innocent people and have ruthlessly ruled this kingdom. They have been judged…by me, to have committed acts of treason and murder. They will be sentenced to death by execution."

The crowd rejoices. The Princess cries, "I love you, father! I love you!"

She can't bear to watch. She tries to find ways to cover her ears but can't. She can hear the swords piercing skin. She hears shrieks of pain from the men. The ghastly screams seem to last an eternity. She hears the slicing of muscle and the cracking of bones. The sounds seem to hang thick in the air like morning fog. She feels sick to her stomach. She wants to throw up. She tries to be strong but cries. She looks for her brother. He's still unconscious. She looks up at the midday sky. The sky is sapphire. The color is so deep it feels like an enormous hole enveloping her. She wants it to swallow her up and to kill her pain. A few streaks of thin white clouds appear in the distance. Evergreen tree tops creep across the view. She closes her eyes. She can't get rid of the sounds. She already thought she lost them. Now, she lost them again. Her heart hurts. It beats fast. It beats faster. She can't breathe. Her crying is deep, and her body heaves with each sob. She wants the pain to stop twisting in her stomach and churning in her chest. She wipes her nose. She takes in a deep breath and whispers, "I love you father. I love you. I'm sorry. It's all my fault."

After several minutes, the Princess is pulled onto her feet. Her brother wakes up, and he is stood up beside her. The woman approaches them and says, "Don't worry, I have some compassion. I won't have you two see their bodies."

The Prince looks at his sister with a puzzled look. She doesn't tell him. The woman says, "Now, should I sentence you two to death? Or should I be more lenient?"

"Who are you?" asks the Princess.

"You'll find out soon enough."

"You've done what you set out to do. Let us be. We can't do you any harm."

The woman laughs. She replies, "My dear, even an ant can do harm. Once, a small boy saw a carpenter ant in his bedroom. The boy was so lonely. He didn't have any friends. He decided the ant would be his pet. He brought the ant a crumb. The ant was happy. And so, every day, several times a day, the boy brought the ant a crumb. The ant never got bigger. The boy figured that was perfect. One morning, the boy woke up to horrific screams. He stepped out of his room. To his surprise, the entire house had fallen down. His father and mother yelled, 'What did you do? Our house is gone!' The boy said he didn't do anything. His father said the house was full of ants, and they had eaten up the whole house except for the boy's room. They ate away the foundation, moved up through the walls and floors, and now devoured the rest."

"We're not ants," replies the Princess.

"Of course, you're not, and neither am I," the woman says and winks.

The woman stands and looks across the crowd. She gestures to the crowd with her long, willowy arms and hands. Her crimson sleeves hang loose and dangle off her forearms. She yells, "What shall we do with the children?"

The crowd screams "kill them" and "torture them". No one shows compassion. They had all been tormented and denigrated by them, especially the Princess. The two children look out at the crowd. The Prince looks for his mother's family but doesn't see them. He wonders what happened to them. The Prince starts breathing hard. He can't take the pressure. He has anxiety and starts to cry. He falls to his knees. The Princess looks over and tries to comfort him. The woman only smiles. She signals to the crowd to quiet down. She says, "Alright, alright. They are only children. We must show some compassion. But we know we can never trust these two. My decision, my sentence then is to transform them and banish them into the Snow Forest."

The crowd is euphoric and cheers. They chant "Snow Forest" over and over. The sound is deafening. The Princess stares out in disbelief. How did this all happen so quickly? The head maid walks up the steps. What is she doing here? The Prince also sees her. He looks at her longingly as if she'll free him. Instead, she scowls at them. She pulls out two stuffed animals and hands them to the woman. She walks away without speaking a word.

The Prince and Princess recognize their favorite stuffed animals. They are bewildered. The woman hands a skinny yellow rabbit to the Princess, and a short chubby white rabbit to the Prince. She says, "I believe these are yours. Your maid tells me they're your favorites. Is that right?"

The two nod.

"Good," says the woman. "What are their names?"

The Prince says, "Annie and rabbit."

The woman sarcastically says, "How appropriate. The Princess named her rabbit after herself."

The two children hold onto their animals for whatever final comfort they can get. The guards drag them up to the front, one on each side of the woman. The woman lifts up her hands and recites an incantation that no one understands. The Prince and the Princess are magically lifted up and hover above the ground. Their fingers and toes tingle, their eyes close, and their stomachs turn all around. They feel nauseous and distorted. They scrunch up their faces in pain. They're dizzy—the world spins faster and faster. Then everything stops, they

29

fall down, and the pain is gone.

They open their eyes. The crowd laughs and screams euphorically.

9. ANNIE & PIKA

"You're a rabbit!" screams the Prince.

"You're a stupid rabbit too!" exclaims the Princess.

The crowd laughs uncontrollably. The Prince and the Princess stare out. They look up and see the guards standing high above them. Their shackles have fallen as well as their clothes. They really have turned into rabbits. With their mouths open, they just stare at one another. Their first instinct is to run away, but they don't. They are paralyzed by bewilderment. They have no idea what to do.

The Prince reaches up to touch the Princess' long yellow ears and the thin black whiskers sticking out from her cheeks. Her black beady eyes are sad. Her belly has azure fur, and her legs and arms are long and skinny. The Princess grabs his face and pulls him in. She stares at his face. His gray-white chubby cheeks and short stubby limbs have erased all his athleticism. His round furry ears droop over his face. She looks at his big bubbly blue eyes filling up with tears and hugs him tight.

Grabbing them by the ears, the woman holds them up. All the villagers clap and cheer. The Prince and the Princess look out at the crowd, and they can't believe what's happened. They are still in shock and can't talk. The woman whispers to the Princess, "You asked who I am earlier. I'm Empress Wu. You never leave an ant alive. You crush it with your foot, twisting and pressing it until you're certain it's dead."

The woman laughs and drops the rabbits. Then the children are

31

shocked. They see Master Tao approach. He plucks them up and tosses them into a bag with small holes. The woman yells, "Off to Snow Forest!"

A roar erupts from the crowd. The Prince and the Princess peer out of the tiny holes at the only world they've known. They hug one another as they bounce around in the bag.

Master Tao carries the bag with him down the corridor and out to the stable. He throws the bag over the saddle and mounts the hazelnut horse. A few other men join him. They ride off through the tunnel which opens into Harmony Meadow.

The Prince and the Princess bounce against the horse's ribs. They see Master Tao's cloth slippers through the holes. Their palace disappears in the distance, and they watch the passing tall grass of Harmony Meadow.

The horses gallop fast. The kids bounce up and down in the bag. The Princess sickens from all the bouncing. Her cheeks turn pink. She holds her stomach and tries to find a way to stay still. The Prince says, "Just don't throw up in here. I don't want to be sitting in your vomit."

"Shut up," growls a sickly Princess.

"It's all your stupid fault."

"Whatever. Just shut up."

The Prince looks out again. He tries to rip the hole bigger, but his paws can't get a good grip. He's clumsy with his rabbit hands and body. He holds his belly, lets go and watches it jiggle around. He winces and whines, "Ugh, this sucks. This is so bad. I'm fat, and I can't move. It's like being in a giant bowl of jelly."

"Stop talking. You're making me more sick."

"Just look out the holes. You can't just look inside here."

The Princess peers out a hole. She sees the setting sun, casting a dry, bright light across the burnt lime-colored grass. The forest is approaching, faster and faster. Her heart beats faster and faster, almost in time with the horse's pounding hooves. She looks at the guards in their dented and war-torn armor. She notices her father's emblem still on them—a crowned dragon wrapping itself around the sun. She gets mesmerized by the guards' horses galloping legs, circling around and around and around. BLEGH!!

"Ewwww!" yells the Prince. He does his best to scoot back in the bag away from the puke. Most of the barf flies out the holes, but a few traces roll around at the bottom of the bag. He scrambles and sticks his paws into nearby holes to keep him above the mess.

"Shut up! Leave me alone," exclaims the Princess. She keeps her eyes against the hole. She feels better. Her feet are dirty. Ugh, she thinks. She can't wait till they get to wherever they're going, and she can take a bath.

As they enter Snow Forest, Master Tao calls for his troops to stop. He dismounts. Although his head and body look like two boxes set on top of one another, he moves with the grace and silence of a tiger. He's never been one to wear armor and military gear. The guards dismount and bring out their food. They lean against logs, stretching out their legs, and look out at a small creek. The men drink from the cool waters and eat pork sandwiches. They laugh about their victory, and the older ones brag about old conquests. Master Tao sits on a log in silence. Chewing his sandwich slowly, he stares out into the forest. He takes a break from eating and scratches his bald head. He feels a hair and yanks it out. He flosses his teeth with it.

Master Tao stands and takes the rabbits out of the bag. He ties their ankles to the log, throws them some bread and says, "Eat. This may be your last bit of food for a long time."

The Prince grabs two handfuls of bread and starts to eat. He motions to Master Tao that he's thirsty. The Master provides slack in the rope, and the Prince hops over to the creek for a drink. The Princess doesn't know what to do. She stares at the bread. She still hasn't accepted her destiny and refuses to eat food off the ground. Master Tao sees her and laughs. "Ha! You won't eat? You're too good for it? I see how it is. Such a spoiled girl. I predict you will die in two days. If some animal doesn't eat you, you'll starve from pettiness and pretentiousness. Your brother on the other hand...may last a week. He's much tougher than you. He's a good boy. I wish he didn't suffer this fate. No one does."

She grimaces and glares at him. She hops up to him and kicks his shin. He barely notices. She asks, "Why are you doing this? Who is that woman? How did she change? Is she a witch?"

He looks down at her and chews his sandwich. He smiles and answers, "It's a long story. It's a good story because it shows karma does exist—never do anyone harm, you never know who they are."

"Why are you doing this?" asks the Princess again as she tries a bite of the bread. The dirt is grainy and disgusting—she spits it out.

He laughs. "Come over here Prince. You should hear this too.

Your father did a very evil deed years ago. On Cloud Mountain, there is a shrine named Rain Temple. The most honorable monks across our land live there. They live in peace and harmony."

"Why didn't you live there?" asks the Prince.

"I'm not worthy. I'm a warrior. I'm trained in the practice as a warrior, not as a peace-seeker."

"Why?"

Master Tao leans in to the Prince and pats his head. He replies, "We all choose our paths. Sometimes, you don't realize you've chosen a path until you're well on your way."

"Why don't you change?"

"You are your mother's son," notes Master Tao, smiling at the Prince. He continues, "Sometimes, a destination leads people down a path; other times, a journey leads people down a path. I chose the former. I live with my choice. As I was saying, there is this temple on Cloud Mountain. Your father had heard of this temple all his life. He never thought much of it. Villagers from all around make pilgrimages to this temple for cures, blessings, advice and many other reasons. Only one of these monks, however, was a woman, Master Wu. Many people came to see her specifically because she specialized in cures and magic spells…as you two experienced."

He takes a drink of water. The Princess asks, "What does this have to do with us? This temple is so far away. I've never even heard of it."

"Patience child. I'll get there. So, this temple existed for thousands of years. Its location is a mystery. People find it through hardship, toil and trial. We only know it resides on Cloud Mountain. Most people can't even recall how they found it because it's so hidden.

"All around Cloud Mountain are little villages. Over many generations, people have found ways to build homes in caves and on mountain ledges. Look up. It's hard to see anything up there. But if you squint and peer through the clouds, you'll feel hundreds of eyes watching you. All these villagers endure harsh weather and barren living—they are as tough as they come.

"In the fifteenth year of your father's reign, several villages didn't show up to the Dragon Sun Festival to celebrate his birthday. An illness had spread throughout the mountain villages—children were dying. The parents grew fearful. They'd never seen anything like it. The children grew sick over night with high fevers. Their skin turned purple. Their eyes rolled back, and then they would die. The parents decided to seek out the monks to find a cure. Instead of celebrating your father's birthday, many of them headed into the mountains.

"This transgression offended your father. They showed they valued these monks over your father, who, being the Emperor, is supposed to be the most important person in the world. They chose other people over him. He believed they should've come to him and ask for a miracle. He ordered his army to find this temple and to kill all the monks. Your mother, the Empress, disagreed. She came from the village and knew what this temple meant to the people. She begged him to let it go, but he wouldn't. He was obsessed with being treated like a god. She, herself, loved the Rain Temple. At first, General Sun disagreed and tried to convince your father to relent. In the end, General Sun consented and led the troops into the mountains.

"This land is treacherous, and no one knows exactly where the temple is. Many people have died searching for it. On this quest, many troops died, falling off cliffs or being swept away by rivers." Master Tao takes a break to drink some water and to take a few bites of his sandwich. His troops sit back against the log next to him. His rich baritone voice and calm demeanor make him a great storyteller, and everyone wants to listen.

The Prince says, "I remember this time. My father roamed the palace in frustration. He talked to himself a lot. This was only a few years ago. I was still pretty young. But I remember."

Master Tao nods and continues, "What he did goes down as the most horrible thing any man—let alone, any Emperor—has ever done. Your Mother died from heartbreak. She never wanted to marry him, and this horrible act convinced her how horrible he was. General Sun and his troops found the temple. The night before, they camped below the temple. The monks never knew what was coming. It wasn't fair. That morning, as the monks slept, the army came in and slaughtered them all. The monks who awoke tried to fight. But they were peaceful people. Although they were trained kung fu masters, they chose a different journey than masters like myself. General Sun came upon Master Wu. He kicked and beat her like a dog. Blood seeped out of the cuts on her forehead and chin. Her right arm laid limp and broken on the ground. She curled up to ease the pain in her bruised back and stomach. Her eyes were swollen. He left her there to watch her people die. He told her to tell the people a message 'Emperor Yan is the son of Heaven, and the only one they should worship'. She watched him walk away. She shut her eyes and listened to her friends scream and die."

Master Tao stops. He sighs and takes a deep breath. The Princess is quiet but doesn't seem affected. The Prince is crying and wipes his tears. The Prince says, "I'm sorry for what he did."

The Master nods and says, "What's done is done. Now we let life play itself out."

The Prince walks over to the creek and watches the water rippling around the rocks and gravel. He thinks about all the innocent people killed. He remembers his mother being upset, and now he understands why. He also wonders if this drove his mother to her death. He is filled with anger, but not hatred, towards his father. The Prince looks down into the waters and sees his reflection. Touching his furry ears, he stares and sees his new self for the first time. Dumbfounded, he stops thinking and falls onto his bottom.

The Princess touches his shoulder and motions him to come back. She asks, "Master Tao, did she come back to seek revenge?"

"Yes."

"But you don't just become a warrior overnight. There's also something that doesn't make sense. When she was holding me up, she said, 'I'm Empress Wu.' Why would a monk call herself an empress?"

Master Tao replies, "She wasn't always a monk. We all meet people at a point in their lives. Never assume you know how they arrived at this point. Life itself is a journey, not a destination. When you choose to live life as a destination as I have, you will need to learn to live with disappointment. When you live life as a journey, you'll learn the skills to experience it fully."

"Whatever, I don't get it. Why would she call herself an empress? Is that what she wanted to be?"

"Did your father ever tell you about the last dynasty?"

"The last Empress was horrible. She burned my father's village on the other side of the mountains. She ..." The Princess stops.

Master Tao sees she just came to the realization that Empress Wu was the previous ruler. He looks at the Prince. He also understands. Master continues, "I was living in Dragon Desert. News about the battle got to me. I rode all day only to find the temple burning and the monks murdered. I was empty and hollow inside. I guess you could say I felt dead inside. The only feeling I had was one of anger—I wished I could've defended the temple.

"When I walked into the temple's chamber, Master Wu laid on the rock-strewn floor. I felt her breath on my cheek and carried her to a bench. In short time, I found eight more monks who were still alive but barely. I took care of them all, treating and restoring them all to health. While they rested, I cleaned the temple and removed the rubble. Those were long days and nights. The monks cried in pain. They were tortured by horrible nightmares of the attack.

"As the months passed, the villagers came back and helped me farm, clean and bring life back to the temple. We swore to restore the temple, its reputation and our practice. We rebuilt the temple in two years, and monks from neighboring temples started to join our practice. A year ago, we decided it was time."

"Time for revenge?" asks the Prince. "But it's not in the views of the monks."

"Yes," answers Master Tao. "It's not in their practice to seek revenge, but I'm not of their practice, and Master Wu came from a different life. She had been destroyed by your father twice now. The first time, she learned her ways and forgave. The second time, he ordered the massacre of innocent, peaceful lives. She couldn't forgive that."

Master Tao stands, stretches his arms and legs, and walks to the creek and back. The guards also stand and stretch. They know the rest of the story. They check their horses and packs, and prepare to leave shortly. Master Tao continues, "Five of us left the temple for the palace and lived in the village. I came from the same village as your father. In the past, I held him in high regard. After the massacre, I saw him differently. I asked him to be your teacher. He took me for my word. We all believed your mother would've made an honorable and fair Empress. But then she died from grief. We had to change our plans.

"We took our time to build up the villagers' support. Then, when you two visited the village the other day, it was the perfect opportunity to show the people what evil you have brought upon this kingdom. You, my princess, so wrongly abused a little boy and an old woman, that we didn't have to do anything—it was so clear in everyone's mind that a rightful leader would never treat her people that way. People should be treated equally and fairly."

The Princess is shocked. She shakes her head. She yells, "I was set up! You all framed me!"

"No princess, you set yourself up. No one had to do anything. You did it all yourself."

"No! You set me up!" She reaches out to hurt the Master. The guards approach, but he gestures them back. He pushes her back down easily.

"Princess, you're not going to survive for very long."

The Prince looks at his sister with disdain. He says, "Sister, you did it yourself. Open your eyes. You brought all this on us. Father's dead. General's dead. Open your eyes!"

"People are useless! You're useless! People don't know anything. You all need me to show you the truth," she exclaims.

"Listen to yourself," says Master Tao. "Who thinks like that? Who would follow someone like that?"

"Shut up!" yells the Princess. She turns her back and hunches over her knees. She cries. She grabs her long yellow ears.

The Prince looks up at Master Tao. He approaches him and whispers, "I'm sorry."

Master Tao is surprised and looks at him. He nods. Then he replies, "I'm sorry for you. Your mother would've been proud of you."

Master Tao stands up and motions the guards to leave. He puts the rabbits in a new bag and throws them over the horse's saddle again. They ride through the forest. The sun is nearly gone, and its golden rays struggle to find their way through the thick forest like fingers foraging through mud. The forest floor changes from a dusty pale sienna color to an orange-tan glow. The trail leads them through trees and up a dusty gravel path. Soon the trees change from cedars to oaks and firs. They ascend a mountain, and the rabbits can see the treetops below them. The temperature drops ten degrees, and the trees give way to rocky cliffs and drab shrubs.

The sound of a waterfall gets louder and louder. They stop. Master Tao dismounts and grabs the bag. He sets the rabbits down by a waterfall pool. He fills the bag with bread and carrots. He mounts his horse and says, "For what it's worth, you're in the heart of Snow Forest. This is Mercy Falls. Cloud Mountain is ahead. It's your best chance for survival. You'll know what I mean soon enough. Goodbye, and may the heavens look with mercy on you two."

10. REFLECTION

Osani, the story now becomes familiar. It becomes the one most of us know. But I want you to know the truth and how they came to us. One day, if you do go to the palace, you will know where Annie and Pika came from, especially Annie. I'm not saying you are her, but she once was like you. We all change. When you have others depend on you for survival, you change. Take me—I used to be fun but have grown serious in my age, especially after your mom was born. Really. I'll tell you more about her another night. She was remarkable. I miss her so. Fate is vindictive when you outlive your children.

The Princess stands at Mercy Falls with her eyes shut—the sound of constant crashing water pounds and pounds every thought out of her mind like giant waves propelling rocks and sands off a beach. Prince Pika comes back from roaming and scouting the area.

"What are we going to do?" asks the Prince.

"I don't know."

"It's dusk. It'll be dark soon. We need to find shelter. We'll freeze to death."

"I know."

"Where should we go?"

"I don't know."

The Prince gets frustrated. His sister is paralyzed by fear and indecision. She just stands staring at the waterfall. High in the air, dozens of streams spew over ledges, colliding into one another, cascading into one wide curtain of white water and crashing into behemoth charcoal boulders. Exploring the area, he looks for fallen logs and rock holes. He spots two logs that fell onto one another, making a canopy. Finding his sister in the same place, he says, "Come on, I found a place."

"No, I want to stay here."

"We can't. It's going to get dark soon. Animals will be out. It'll be freezing cold. We have to go. I found a place."

She nods and follows him. She looks at the logs and disgustingly says, "This? You expect me to stay here? Sleep on the dirt? This is filthy. The trees are rotten."

The Prince gets mad. "Look! All you do is abuse me and everyone else! You're not doing anything. We're stinking rabbits! It's all your fault! Father's dead because of you! And you're too stupid to even realize that! We're all alone now. We only have each other. And you're too conceited to even know that, and you're too stupid to know we're going to die! What's wrong with you?!"

"Shut up! How dare you speak to me like that!" she yells back.

"That's it! I'm out of here." With his two strong hind legs, the Prince leaps over the logs and runs off.

The Princess watches him leave. She tells herself he'll be back. She sits on the logs waiting. He never returns. The world is dark. She hears the constant crashing of the cascading water. The moonlight glimmering off the water provides a little ambient light.

Although starving and thirsty, she refuses to drink from the waterfall and the creek. She can't remember where the general put the bag of bread. She just sits by the waterfall. Soon, animal noises fill the nighttime air with sounds she's never heard before—hoots and howls, barking and bellowing. She's scared to death. She shakes from both cold and fear. She stays by the water because she doesn't trust the darkness in the trees and the forest. Soon, the weather grows cold and damp. "Pika, where are you?!" she finally yells. He never answers nor comes back.

She doesn't sleep that night. Every sound keeps her awake and frightens her—beetles crawling, twigs snapping, leaves crunching, bushes bristling. Something is watching her, she believes. She doesn't know if it's reality or her mind. She doesn't trust herself anymore. "What's happening to me?" she asks herself. She tries to be strong and confident, but it's no use. She only thinks of what she just hears, what she just sees, what she just feels, and what she just wants.

In the moonlight, she spots a boulder in the water. That'll be the safest spot for her. She shakes and trembles from the damp cold and fear. She hugs herself to stay warm. She stands near the water. She dabs her toe and shrieks, "That's so cold!"

She covers her mouth in surprise. She's scared of any animals hearing her. She touches the water again and screams. She runs back to the shrubs on the shore. She huddles and tries to stay warm. All of a sudden, she cries uncontrollably. Her father's dead. Was that a tiger behind her? The General's dead. Her mother's dead. Was that a bat? Her brother hates her. It's so cold. Her mind can't stop racing. She just wants to die. This is horrible. She can't die this way. She's the Princess. It's so cold. Her stomach's growling. It's so loud. Her tongue is dry—her throat too. Was that an eagle far away? Or just a baby crying? It's so cold. It's so cold. Nature is all around her, and all she sees are dark eyes watching her.

Although she swears thousands of animals sniffed her, blew at her, and ran by her, I doubt anything really did. The sun peeks its rays out from above the mountains, and the sunlight pours into the canyon of the waterfall. The sunlight feels warm on her damp fur. She's still shaking. She must be sick. Her heart is pounding. Her mind is wound up. She can't relax.

She looks at Mercy Fall coming over the crescent rocks high above her. The water continues to pour out. It poured yesterday. It poured

41

last night. It pours this morning. And it'll pour for eternity. Then she realizes she's going to die…probably tonight. She doesn't know how to eat, how to find shelter and how to survive. Master Tao was right— she's going to die in two days. She's starving, and she can't bring herself to drink from the creek or eat the leaves off these trees. What's wrong with her?

Worst of all, she's alone. No one's going to know she's dead. She treated her brother so poorly, and now he's gone. He's the only person left in this world who would care. Her mother's dead. Her father's dead. The General's dead. Master Tao's a traitor. There's no one left. No one knows where she is. No one cares. She stops. She finally realizes that no one cares about her. She hunches over her knees, shuts her eyes and cries uncontrollably. She can't wipe her tears away fast enough. She opens her eyes and sees the tears have created a pool of mud under her legs. She stands up and walks over to the waterfall pool.

She dips her hands in. The water is freezing cold, but it feels good. She washes her hands, and then throws water on her face. She jumps—the cold water splashing on her face shocks her senses. The ice-cold water sends a chill down her spine. She shakes it off. She goes back to the pool. She notices her reflection.

"I'm…I'm a rabbit," she mutters. She touches her face, her ears, and her whiskers. It's the first time she's seen herself. She forgot she had been cast into a rabbit. Through the nightmare of last night, she forgot that it's even worse than she was thinking—she's a stupid rabbit!

She falls to her knees in the pool of water. Then she falls on her bottom, sitting and wallowing in the pool. She doesn't care. Life doesn't mean anything anymore. She heaves a deep heavy sigh.

11. MERCY FALLS

"Wake up, wake up," gently says the Prince while prodding the Princess.

She rolls around and grunts. He prods her again. She blinks her eyes and sees a chubby white-gray rabbit staring at her. "Aggghhh!" she screams. She jumps up and trips backwards. "Get away!"

"What are you talking about? It's me, Pika."

"What?" she says, shaking her head. Then she realizes it wasn't a bad dream. She's a rabbit. Pika's a rabbit. They're lost in the forest. She looks at him and can't believe he came back. She runs over and hugs him tight.

He hugs her back. She's never really hugged him, and he appreciates it. "Are you okay?" he asks.

"Yes. I mean 'no'." She takes a hold of his shoulders. "Let me look at you…you silly rabbit."

Hugging him again, she forgets her hunger and her chills. She pushes him back and turns him around to look him over. It's the first time she's really looked at him, especially as a rabbit. She laughs, "Not too bad. You make a sort of cute chubby rabbit."

"Yeah, you're a skinny yellow rabbit. Kind of suits you," he replies, enjoying this new playfulness with his sister. "Did you eat?"

"No, I forgot where the bag was."

"You didn't try some plants?"

"No, I couldn't bring myself to…"

"Of course, you couldn't." He smiles. He hops over a few shrubs and finds Master Tao's bag. He comes back.

"It was right there the whole time?"

"Yes," he replies. They both laugh.

The Prince rations out some bread to eat. He shows the Princess some tricks he learned overnight—he hops and performs a backflip, he jumps several body-lengths into the air, and he leaps across the creek. While he scratches his back with his hind foot, the Princess laughs.

After they finish eating, she asks, "Where were the logs you found? You're right. We should use it as shelter. Where did you stay last night?"

"I met some animals, and we stayed in a nearby rock stack. They told me what to look out for, and how to get around." He pauses and then adds, "I think I made a friend."

"What? Really?"

"Yes, her name is Naso. She's a long-eared jerboa," he says.

"A what?"

"She's a dusty white and gray mouse with big ears and big feet and a long tail. She can jump super far. She's hilarious. A little crazy, but very nice. She's sleeping now. She comes out at night and sleeps during the day."

Yes, Osani, I know what you're thinking. Yes, that's me, and where I come into the story. Just wait, I'll get there soon enough. I'm old, so let me tell the story how I like to tell it. I'm set in my ways. It's hard to change.

The Princess asks, "How'd you meet her?"

"It's funny. We bumped into each other. I was looking for a place to sleep. She was looking for some bugs to eat. We both were searching in the rocks. Our heads hit. We laughed, and then we started talking. She lost her parents a long time ago, and she's been living around Mercy Falls ever since. She doesn't remember much because she was so young. I told her our story. It's kind of the same when you think about it. We're all starting out here. I told her I'd find you, and we can meet up tonight."

"That sounds nice."

"If you meet her..."

"What do you mean 'if'?" interrupts the Princess.

"I mean I have to ask you something."

"What?"

"You can't be mean."

"I'm not mean," says the Princess.

"Yes, you are."

"No, I'm not. You're the mean one."

He stares at her and knows his answer. She sees his look, and she remembers last night. She exhales. "Ok, it's hard for me to do this," she starts and looks away. She pauses for a long time and continues, "It's hard...so hard. Ok, look, I'm kind of sorry. I kind of treated you horribly, especially last night."

Pika falls back. He's shocked and surprised. He scrambles back to his feet. He stammers, "What? What?"

The Princess paces around and doesn't make eye contact. She's nervous and clasps her hands. "Look, I'm sorry. I wasn't very nice to you."

He realizes how hard it's for her to say this. He walks up to her and gives her a hug. She hugs him back. He says, "Thank you, sis. Please be nice to Naso. She's nice. She's my friend."

45

He pauses and then adds, "My first real friend."

"I'll do my best."

"She told me a secret."

"What?"

"There's a unicorn that lives over the mountains."

"A unicorn? Aren't they make believe?" the Princess asks.

"They're rare, she says. If you find a unicorn, they can break magic spells or grant a wish."

"We can be human again?"

"Yes."

"We have to find this unicorn."

"We don't know where to find it."

"Naso can help us, right?"

"Only if we're friends."

"We'll be friends."

"We have to be real friends," he adds.

"Yes," she says. She looks up at the sun shining above the waterfall and the water spilling down into the pool. The cool mist hitting her face feels refreshing. Today feels so different than last night. She was certain death was imminent, and now, she feels completely refreshed…hopeful.

12. NASO

Pika and the Princess sit in a field of rocks near the waterfall. The bag of food is slung over Pika's back. The Princess is feeling happy. She sits close to her brother. The two of them watch the sun setting over the top of the waterfall. The light slowly crawls out of the canyon like a slug up a mound of dirt. The Princess isn't scared.

Pika says, "Naso will wake up soon. Remember, be nice."

"I know, I get it. Don't worry."

As the last traces of sunlight leap off the rim of the waterfall, with my big giant ears and my long tail bouncing around, I leap up the hill, hopping across the different rocks.

It's funny talking about myself. I have good memories of those days. I was young, and I always had a big smile. I didn't have any responsibilities. And my hair! You should've seen it. It was so rich and full. It was red-yellow like a beautiful sunset. Just like yours Osani. Not like the dusty stone gray white hair I have now. My long, strong paws helped me grasp, balance and propel myself. The Princess was astounded by my jumping ability.

"Hello! You must be Princess Annie," I say.

"Yes, and you must be Naso."

We bow our heads in respect. Mind you, I'm only the size of her palm, although my tail is probably half her length. She's amazed that I'm not blown away by the slightest wind. My tiny little pink nose quivers. My pink lips look like spring painted on. And my deep ebony eyes look like oceans. What, Osani? Oh please. Let me remember my youth with fondness. I'm old and wrinkled now. All my beauty is gone. Look at my lips. They're so dry and gray like these old rocks here.

Anyway, the Princess squats down and asks, "How long have you been here?"

"Time? Who counts time? We live, and we die. Just enjoy! Be here!" I answer in my voice like chimes.

"Do you remember anything before you got here?" she persists in asking.

"Stop it, sis. Do you want her to be sad?" says Pika.

"It's okay," I reply. "Not really. I barely remember my parents. We were escaping a forest fire, and I got separated from them."

"I'm sorry."

"It's alright. It's been a long time now. There's nothing I can do."

"We lost our parents too."

"I heard. I'm sorry too."

The three of us pause for a moment. Pika asks, "Do you want some food? We have bread and carrots."

"Oh yes, I'd love to try some bread. I've heard about it. The golden monkeys once found some. They stole it out of a human's bag when he wasn't looking. They said it was deeeee-licious," I excitedly say. I nibble and nod approvingly. I take a big bite and fall down. I yell, "Yummm!"

One of these days, Osani, you'll have a chance to try some bread. It's sweet and tangy. Not chalky and bitter like this dirt. I chew and smile at the Princess. The Princess smiles back and looks around. Pika looks up and then back down at his feet. It's silent except for my chewing. I take another bite and chew even more loudly. I start to giggle. I want to break the silence, so I take another bite and start chomping. BUUUURRP!

I exclaim, "Come on! You two are so serious. It's so quiet. It's freaky. Like a funeral."

Pika and Princess start to laugh. With my fingers, I pull my mouth open and stick out my tongue. Pika sticks his ear in his mouth. The three of us fall over laughing. The Princess looks at us and then tries to tie her ears. Pika and I laugh because we see how hard the Princess is trying to relax and have fun.

I swing my tail over a low hanging branch on a nearby shrub, my tail wraps around it, and I swing around. I make monkey sounds and pretend to eat a banana. I drop down and laugh. "This is what it's all about—having fun with your friends!"

The Princess wipes away tears of laughter. She dries her eyes. She sits down on the rock. She asks, "Naso, what do you usually do?"

"This, I guess. Each evening, I wake up and eat a couple of bugs. I run around these rocks. If I run into a friend, we'll chat and play. I love to play!"

I pull on the Princess' long ears and let them go—the ears spring back up. We all laugh. I say, "I don't know. I'll find more bugs later. Most of my friends fall asleep by then, so I spend the nights alone."

"Are you lonely?" asks the Princess.

"No, I'm alone, but not lonely," I reply matter-of-factly.

"That's good," she says and pauses. She adds, "I think I get lonely."

"Why?"

Pika just sits and listens. He looks at his sister. She answers, "I don't know. We live in this grand palace, but there aren't many people. There aren't any children. The Prince and I are just there...I don't know if it really matters that we're there."

It's silent again. It's awkward. I get anxious. My eyes move side to side. I'm trying to think of something to say. "I know. Most of the animals at night are owls and wolves and all these other animals that want to eat me. At least, no one's trying to eat you. Can you imagine? I was so happy to meet Pika. And now you!"

The Princess smiles. She thinks about what she just said. She hadn't thought about it before. She just said what popped into her mind. She realizes it was true. Last night changed her. It didn't matter that her brother and her lived in the palace. No one cares now. Her father ruled the kingdom, not them. She looks at her brother. She looks at me. She asks, "Naso, can you find me some food?"

"Sure, what do you like?"

"Why did you agree?"

"We're friends. Why wouldn't I?"

The Princess smiles. She looks at her brother again. "Yes, we're friends. This is nice."

Pika smiles too. He walks over to his sister and says, "Annie." Saying her name catches her off guard. He continues, "Annie, please stop calling me Prince or Crown Prince. It doesn't matter. We're family. I'm just Pika. This is all we have now."

The Princess asks, "Naso, how old are you?"

"I'm not sure. I don't track time. Animals don't do that. We just live in the moment. Your life's journey is more important. Some old animals seem like children, some children seem like wise elders. Does it matter?"

"I suppose not. Where did you live before?"

"I used to live down in Snow Forest with all the other jerboas. One day, a fire burned through the forest. My family was sleeping, and our flying squirrel friends woke us up. They screamed for us to get out. My dad led us, and my mom brought up the rear to make sure none of us kids were lost. I had eight brothers and sisters."

Pika asks, "Are you the oldest?"

"No, I was the second youngest."

"Where are your brothers and sisters?"

Turning quiet, I hunch over and mumble, "They're dead. At least, I think they're dead."

Yes, one day, Osani, I'll tell you more about all your family—your grand uncles and grand aunts, your uncles and aunts, and our large, large family. I miss them dearly. I don't think you ever stop missing them. You just learn to take the best of who they are and make them a part of you.

I'm not sure how, but they got me to talk about my family. It turned so serious. Not sure how. But I felt close to them, so I didn't mind. And so, I continued on with them, "We were heading up the mountain. My father wanted to get above the fire. He thought it was the right way to go. Most of the other animals were heading out into the meadow. The fire and the smoke were getting worse. We couldn't see more than two or three jerboas in front of us. The smoke was the hardest for me. I couldn't breathe. It was hard to run. Trees fell. Embers flew in our faces. The smoke also burned my eyes. Plants burned. It was daytime, but it was dark. As we climbed up boulders to get to Cloud Mountain, a burning tree cracked and fell in front of me, killing two of my brothers. My father and sisters were on the other side. My mother and younger brother were next to me. We couldn't stop to mourn my brothers. We didn't have time. I told my mom I'd help them over the top. I pushed them up. The tree was hot. When I started to climb up, an ember burst. The trunk ignited. I was thrown back. My head landed hard against a boulder. I heard my mom scream for me. I knew they couldn't wait for me. If they tried to save me, they'd die. I yelled to them to leave. The last thing I heard was my mom and dad yelling 'We love you Naso!'. I yelled back I loved them."

Sorry, Osani, give me a moment. I still get sad when I remember that day. You never forget the moment you realize you won't see your loved ones again. I know you understand. It was like that when your parents were lost. Let me hug you. It's alright. Don't worry, the story gets better.

13. UNICORNS & SPIRITS

The three of us spend the evening swimming in the pools of the fall. Afterwards, we sit on the rocks, drying off and talking about Snow Forest. The entire time I can tell the Princess is only half-listening. She wants to ask me something, so I ask, "What's on your mind?"

"What do you mean?"

"I can tell you're thinking about something."

"I'm just thinking about my parents and our life before."

"No, you're not. I can tell you want to ask me something. Ask. Go on."

The Princess looks at her brother. He shrugs. She asks, "I want to learn about the unicorn. Does it really exist? Does it really have magic? Where can we find it?"

I get excited. "I knew it! I'm very intuitive. Pika, did you see that? I was right."

"Can you tell us?" the Princess asks.

"Of course. Unicorns do exist, but they are spirits."

"Spirits?"

"Yes, each kingdom is ruled and protected by an animal spirit. Big ones, little ones, scary ones, cute ones. All different kinds. Some spirits are wanderers. They simply live to travel from kingdom to kingdom. They live in peace. We also have spirits, who want to conquer us. There aren't many spirits, but they live amongst us animals. Most animals are just living life. Some animals focus on reaching a state of purity that they transform into spirits."

Pika says, "Pretty similar to humans."

"I wouldn't know. I haven't really seen any humans."

"There are good people, and there are bad people."

"Is it that clear?"

"What do you mean?"

"Are people only good and only bad? Or are they a mix?"

"I guess they're a mix."

"For us, good and bad are relative. Most of the time, it comes down to good choices and evil choices. Some animals make more harmful choices than good ones, but it doesn't necessarily mean they're bad animals. If you say there are good and there are bad, what are you and the Princess?"

"I don't know. I think we're good," he pauses. "But I suppose other people think we're bad. That's why we're here. They got rid of us. They killed our father."

At this time, I get nervous and am hesitant to speak. I wonder what type of people or rabbits they are. I wonder if I'm going to get into trouble. I give them my famous one-eyed glare. Pika sees this stare. He says, "Don't worry. We're ok. We used to be mean, but we've learned. Right Annie?"

The Princess leans over and says, "Yes, Pika was always better than me. I was horrible. But I'm different now...at least, I'm trying to change."

I simply nod and continue, "Like I said, it's not really about good and bad animals, and good and bad spirits—it's about choices. We all make choices, good ones and hurtful ones. We're all just mixed up bags of rocks. What you pull out of it doesn't mean that's what's all in the bag. There are big rocks, little rocks, pebbles. I guess pebbles are rocks. Sometimes you find twigs and old leaves. Maybe even some caterpillars."

Pika laughs, "You're rambling now."

The Princess asks, "So what kingdom are we in now? Who's the ruling spirit?"

"We're at the foothills of Cloud Mountain just at the edge of Snow Forest. Moyen the Tiger rules Snow Forest."

"How far does it stretch?"

"All around. Moyen's built a massive kingdom. He only has Cloud Mountain and Dragon Desert left to conquer. He's heartless and unforgiving. Most of us have moved into these mountains to live."

Pika asks, "Is it just him?"

I reply, "He has a general. His name is Mantchu. He's a brown-eared pheasant."

"A pheasant?" asks Pika. He holds back his laughter.

"Yes, a pheasant. Don't laugh. He's the smartest and most brilliant animal you'll ever meet. At least we think he is. He talks nonsense— since Moyen listens to him, we figure he must be very smart. He's also very loyal to Moyen. The two of them live and roam the forests, but they continue to move around to ensure everyone's in line. Moyen rules ruthlessly. Any animal who argues or disputes him is killed. He doesn't tolerate most animals. He just seems to want more and more, and nothing pleases him."

Pika and the Princess look at one another. Moyen sounds like their father, and even the Princess. She asks me, "Do the other animals like him?"

"No, many times the animals have revolted. Each time, he's fought them back. He continues to grow his army. It gets harder to stop them," I reply shaking my head. "Animals can't kill spirits; only a spirit can kill another spirit."

The Princess looks down. She knows this story. "Naso, I'm sorry. I understand what you're all going through. I also understand him. How are things now?"

"It's getting worse. We're all starving. There's talk of another revolution. This may be it. The animals are restless. They've enlisted the help of Leuca, our living mountain spirit. He's reluctant, but he knows it's necessary. Onensis, the red-crowned crane, is the spirit of Cloud Mountain. But between us, he's scared and afraid of dying. I'm not sure how he became a spirit, but he did. He's tricked Leuca to stop his wandering ways and to lead us. My suspicion is that he's getting Leuca to do the dirty work. It's not right, I tell you. Leuca is peaceful. He's a happy panda. Just wants to wander around and eat bamboo. Peaceful spirits can't be warriors. It just won't work."

The Princess asks, "Do you think it'll happen soon?"

"Probably. They've been training for a long time now. It's getting harder to train without Moyen finding out." I lick my lips. "Alright, I'm hungry. Let's find some food."

"Wait, just one more question," says the Princess. "Where's the unicorn?"

"Ahh, the unicorn. She lives on the other side of Cloud Mountain in Dragon Desert. There are many stories about her. No one knows anyone who's seen her, but we've all heard stories about someone who knows someone who's related to someone who may have talked to someone who may have seen her. Some have been cured by her, others have died; some grew into mighty warriors, others coiled up like worms. It seems there's a story for every occasion. The one I believe is that she only appears when a new spirit arrives or leaves us. I believe this one because I've seen a trail of fire in the sky whenever a spirit has fallen."

The Princess asks, "How do you know it's her?"

"I don't. It's just what I believe. We all need more than ourselves in this world."

"What else do you know about her?"

"Qilin—that's her name—is the mother of all spirits. I don't think any spirit can kill her."

"Are you sure?"

"Nope!" I laugh. I jump up onto a boulder and bounce off my tail. I get bored with the conversation. It had turned so serious. "Come on! This is so serious. I can't take it anymore. Let's go eat!"

"Alright, alright. Just one more question," says the Princess.

"Stop with the questions," I say. "Geez, let's go."

"How is Qilin the mother of all spirits? Why don't you find her to stop Moyen?"

"I don't know. I'm just a jerboa. My place in this world is between these rocks. It's none of my business."

"Do you believe she has magical powers, or she can break spells?"

"Yes," I say hauntingly.

"How?"

"You live long enough to believe and not believe in certain things. Some things can be explained, and others can't." I pause, smile and add in a mysterious voice, "Or maybe, we all need something to believe in…belief gives us a place where fear falls away."

The Princess thinks for a minute and asks, "How can we find her?"

"You need someone to bring you to Dragon Desert. Then you can find her by a dead tree fallen over a stream. I don't know how realistic that is. No one's seen her in my lifetime."

"You just said…"

"I know what I said. Can't you tell that I don't really know what I'm talking about? Come on, let's go," I laugh.

55

"Alright, alright, let's go eat," the Princess says. "But if we don't try to find her, we'll never find a way to break this spell."

"You two look cute. It could've been worse," I say.

Pika laughs and says, "Naso, we have to find this unicorn. We're not rabbits. We don't know how to be rabbits. We won't survive for very long."

"If the humans turned you into rabbits, what makes you think they want you back?" I ask.

"I don't know. We don't have to go back. Or maybe we can show them we changed. I don't know what the answer is. I just want to live. I want my sister to live. We're all we have left. You're the only one who understands what we're going through," pleads Pika.

"Come on, let's go and eat. You'll need a full stomach for your journey."

14. CLOUD MOUNTAIN

In the light of the moon, the three of us scramble across boulders and rocks. We make our way up the mountain trails until we stand at the base of Cloud Mountain. Mercy Falls feels like a distant memory. We're tired, and our paws ache. My front paws have blisters from all the jagged rocks and gravel. I haven't hiked that far in a long time, and my paws aren't used to it. The Princess massages her feet and stretches her wrists. She looks at a cut on her foot. Surprisingly, she hasn't complained. Pika pulls away the fur on his paws and looks the pads of his feet over. The stars are shining bright above and are very clear. The moon is slowly descending.

The Princess gazes up at the black and charcoal cliffs. They rise almost straight up into the sky with no end in sight. She has no idea how we're going to scale them—she's never worked this hard before. The shadow of trees crown the rim of the peaks. A few scattered clouds glow a pearly teal in the moonlight around the peaks.

A strong cold wind blows down from the peaks. We shield our faces. I say, "We'll need to find a place to rest. It's almost time for me to sleep."

The Princess and Pika also want to sleep. They're not used to staying up all night. The Princess replies, "Yes, let's find some safe shelter."

Pika finds a crevice at the base of the peak. We find some twigs to make a bed frame and set leaves on top to make a soft bed. We lay down to sleep. A few stones are stacked to protect the entrance. I still remember my dream that night. I'm not sure why. I was flying through the sky. My brothers and sisters were in front of me, flying too. We all soared and glided up and down all around. The trees were far below, and we glided towards the sun. It got hotter and hotter. Then my fur began to melt, and all the hair started to fall out. I couldn't fly anymore and started falling out of the sky. My brothers and sisters screamed my name, and reached to get me. I fell too fast. My oldest brother pressed his arms against his body and nosedived towards me. As the hair fell out, feathers grew at the end of my tail and on my hands and feet, and dragon-like scales shot across my skin. A thin ridge of scaled fins shot down my back to my tail. My body felt heavier yet lighter—it's so hard to describe. The world started to shrink, and I realized I was falling into a hole. Suddenly, the sky was gone! I was sucked through this hole. It was all white. It was silent. I yelled, "Mom! Dad!" I couldn't hear my voice. Not even an echo came back. I was standing and floating in mid-air at the same time. I felt the whole world was expanding. It was so odd. The room was white, yet I could feel it getting bigger and bigger.

"Wake up," whispers a voice. The voice is screechy and sounds like tin. "Wake up, hurry, wake up."

A small, squirrel-like animal crawls into the crevice. It shakes me. "Naso, wake up!"

I open my eyes. "Bei, what are you doing here? How'd you find me?"

"What are you doing here?"

"We're on our way to the Dragon Desert," I answer.

"Whatever for?"

"To find the unicorn."

"What? Why?"

I look at my friends, I shake my head, and I decide not to explain, "Never mind. What are you doing here?"

"The time has come. Leuca has called a council meeting."

"Really? This is serious." I look at the Princess and Pika, and wake them up. "Princess, Pika. We can't go to the Dragon Desert. We can't search for the unicorn. The time has come."

They are sleepy. The Princess asks, "What are you talking about? What's going on? Who is this?"

I explain, "Leuca has called a council meeting. All animals have to attend. It will be decided whether or not we go to war."

"But...," starts the Princess.

58

"It'll actually be on the way. So, if nothing happens at this meeting, we'll continue on. Or we'll soon discover our new fate."

"Alright," says the Princess. She doesn't want to go, but she shies away from ordering me.

We hike up the mountain. We pass Nine Dragon Falls and Mother-Child Rock. Bei leads the way, leaping from boulder to boulder at an astounding speed. Tired and weary, the rest of us slowly make our way up the mountain. The sound of another waterfall seeps into our ears from around the corner. We are on a small ledge and sidestep our way around the corner. The fog inches in like a cat creeping in on its prey. It's so thick that we can't see more than a few steps in front of us, but we can hear the waterfall getting closer and closer. Suddenly, we step through the fog like a curtain of grass. We welcome the sight of Black Crane Falls rushing off a cliff into a bowl carved into the rocks like a crane swooping into a river for fish. The Princess and Pika stop. A temple carved out of a giant pine stands before us. Beautiful, clear, large openings surround the facade, where it looks out at the waterfall. Bamboo floors line the branches leading you from one chamber to another. Small lanterns light up the paths and windows. There is a serene, tranquil feeling surrounding the temple.

Many animals are making the same pilgrimage. A line of them winds around the mountain from the gate to where we stood. After some time, we are in the temple and walk to the courtyard in the middle of the tree. There is quiet conversation. Everyone is waiting for Leuca to arrive.

Pika and I talk and greet other animals. The Princess sits quietly watching. She feels out of place—she doesn't look like a real rabbit and feels out of place, whereas Pika looks real.

Suddenly, a hush falls over the crowd, and they start moving aside. The Princess sees a red cat-like animal walk in. The animal's ears and mouth are covered in white fur. It has black pearl eyes, a soft black nose and long white whiskers. She asks, "Naso, is that the spirit?"

"No, that's Red—she's his general. Leuca told Onensis he wouldn't consider the leadership without Red. She's his cousin, and the one who actually has battle experience. Leuca is a peaceful spirit. Red is a trained warrior, serious and strict—everyone is scared of her, but in a good way. She is well-respected."

As Red walks in on her furry black paws and ivory claws, she smells something. She stops, sits up, and looks around. She sees the Princess and Pika. Her eyes squint and narrowly cross. She moves on.

The Princess asks, "Was she looking at us?"

"I don't know," I reply.

"I wonder if she knows."

Red approaches and walks up the podium. She motions for everyone to quiet down. Then she turns and looks back. The temple doors open, everyone stands aside, and a giant panda as tall as the chamber walks through. Its large white head and black eyes and ears gaze from side to side. It lumbers in on its thick, strong, black legs. I whisper, "That's Leuca."

The Princess says, "Yes, it's obvious now."

Leuca stands next to Red and speaks. "Friends, the time is approaching where we each face a choice foretelling our own true self. I cannot stand here and tell you, nor ask you, what to do. I cannot stand here and promise a destiny that none of us know. I only can tell you what you already know. The world is large, yet very, very small. Moyen aims to rule this world. He will not rest until he has broken and conquered each and every one of us. That is the destiny he has chosen. That is what he believes will bring him happiness. But

60

happiness is fleeting. It is a moment in time. Our lives are not a single moment, but many moments that comprise a journey. If Moyen achieves his ambition, then each and every one of you has to face the reality that your journeys as you know it today will be altered forever. We all know what that will be. We will be his slaves. He will control the moments of your lives forever. Your freedoms, your choices, your journeys will all be taken away. For this and only this reason, I ask each and every one of you in the most selfish request I've ever had to join me in defeating Moyen."

The crowd erupts in cheers and rejoicing. Leuca motions for everyone to settle down and to quiet. He says, "I hear you. Let it be known that we will join as one to fight as one to win as one. This is our journey together. Let it be so."

You should've seen this crowd—animals hugging, singing and dancing. I'd never seen all these different animals come together—predators and prey, warriors and monks. Times have changed. We no longer have a leader like Leuca. We are all so selfish now. I suppose selfishness comes with the best of times.

After a moment, Red holds up her hands and says, "There are new creatures amongst us."

There is commotion, and animals look around. Animals start noticing the Princess and stand back. Soon a clearing forms around us.

"Come here," says Red. We walk to the podium. Red and Leuca look at us. There is silence.

Leuca asks, "Where are you from?"

The Princess answers, "From Yan Palace."

"You are not animals I would assume," says Leuca. He smells them with his large black nose. "You are humans."

A loud gasp rolls through the crowd. Animals start talking. Leuca says, "Quiet please. I sense they mean us no harm. Is that right?"

"Yes," answers the Princess.

"Who put this spell on you?"

"A woman. She says her name is Empress Wu."

Leuca steps back and grins. "Ahh, Empress Wu. Why did she do this to you?"

"I don't know."

Pika jumps in and says, "She hates us. She killed our father and changed us!"

Leuca leans in and asks, "Why would she do this?"

"She hates us," yells Pika.

The Princess interrupts. "My father destroyed her home and killed her people."

"Ahh, I see," Leuca says. He sits back and thinks. "What was he?"

"The Emperor."

Someone in the crowd yells, "Banish them! They're the enemies. They'll kill us!"

Red yells back, "Quiet! Don't react. Let's hear them out."

Leuca asks, "What are you two doing here?"

"We're on our way to find the unicorn," says the Princess.

"The unicorn? How do you know she exists?"

"We don't. But it's our only hope. We want the spell to be broken, so we can return home."

Leuca asks, "What about us animals and our land?"

"What about you?"

Leuca laughs and leans back. "You're only concerned about yourself, aren't you?"

The Princess is embarrassed and mumbles, "I guess so."

Leuca bellows a hearty, deep laugh. He holds the Princess and Pika with a giant paw. "Alright, I see we have a lot to teach you two. Welcome to Cloud Mountain!"

The crowd is confused and doesn't know how to react. Aren't they at war? Aren't these humans? Why would they help them? Most of them politely applaud.

The Princess and Pika don't know how to react. They are confused. What's going on? Have they just joined the rebellion? What about the unicorn? Can they leave? Leuca looks out at the crowd and exclaims, "Tonight, we celebrate. Play some music!"

15. TRAINING

After a few months, in the middle of fall, one morning, the Princess wakes to find Pika and myself missing. She assumes we already went out to start training—we had been training martial arts for months now. The Princess lays in her bed, staring at the ceiling. She scratches her back. The bed of leaves and twigs itches her. She still isn't used to her new body and living as an animal. She looks around the room.

Red gave us a small room up on a branch overhanging the creek flowing from Black Crane Falls. The room has three small beds made out of leaves and twigs. A round table rests in the middle of the room where we eat and read. Red has all the animals reading a book on the art of war. There are a few wooden boxes for us to keep our belongings, but for the most part, no one has anything. We have to give up material desires to focus on our internal, spiritual struggle. The room has two large openings where we can look out—on one side we see the waterfall; on the other side, we can look out at the courtyard.

The Princess hears commotion outside. She stands up and walks over to the courtyard window. She looks out to see Pika in the middle of a circle of animals. He's facing a golden monkey twice his size. The monkey has red-orange hair with light blue skin around its eyes and mouth. Its eyes are two black holes. It has white ears and a sand-colored stomach. The Princess recognizes him. She doesn't know his name but has seen him in all the training. He's Red's top instructor and student. He often demonstrates new techniques. He's strong, agile and relentlessly brutal.

What's Pika doing? He's been training for a few months and doing well, but he's not ready to fight an experienced warrior. The monkey pokes his shoulder. Pika stands still. The other animals are chanting and calling for a fight. The animals still don't trust Pika and the Princess. They often have conversations about getting rid of them. Where are the teachers and Red? The monkey snarls, showing its sharp teeth. It charges, Pika moves away, and the monkey misses. This one-sided attack continues for several minutes. Pika never retaliates but finds ways to dodge the attacks. The monkey gets frustrated. He leaps up, pounds the ground, and rams head first into Pika. This time, Pika can't dodge the attack. He gets knocked back with his head hitting the ground first. The other animals cheer. Pika is woozy getting up. He feels a bump on the back of his head but doesn't see any blood on his hand. The Princess presses her face against the window. She whispers, "Get up, Pika. Get up."

As Pika stands up, the monkey punches his right cheek, sending Pika wobbling backwards again. The monkey throws its tail to sweep Pika off his feet. Pika hops over the tail. The monkey lunges towards his head. Pika ducks, turns and jumps up to kick the monkey in the chin. Pika spins and throws another kick which cracks the cheek, and the monkey falls to the ground. Grabbing the monkey's tail, Pika twirls the monkey in circles and throws him. The monkey crashes head first into the wall. Pika leaps over and slams his shoulder into the monkey's stomach, and the monkey lets out a deep groan. The monkey lays motionless on the ground. Pika walks away, and the crowd opens up to let him through. A silence falls over the crowd. The Princess rushes out the room, down the corridor and stairs, and searches for Pika. She finds him and hugs him tight. She asks, "Are you alright?"

He nods.

"What happened? Why did he fight you?"

Pika shrugs her off and walks over to the meditation room. He sits down and closes his eyes. The Princess walks over. "What happened? I don't want you to fight."

"I have to. It's all we have now."

The Princess grabs his shoulders and says, "No, we're all we have. I only have you, and you only have me. I can't have anything happen to you. I can't."

Pika looks at her and says, "Don't worry, sis. I had it under control."

At this point, I walk in all happy and smiling. The Princess asks me, "What happened?"

"Rhino picked the wrong fight."

"Rhino? That monkey? Why?"

"Jealousy. All the animals are jealous that a human can master the traditional fighting skills so quickly. They're also jealous that Pika is becoming Leuca's favorite."

"But why is Rhino picking a fight? Isn't he supposed to be the teacher?" asks the Princess.

"Rhino was raised to be our great warrior. He's been Onensis' favorite. When Leuca became our leader, Rhino fell out of favor because he's so violent. Rhino's been mad for a while. He just used Pika as an excuse."

"It's not Pika's fault."

"No, it's just nature." I give Pika a hug and see a grasshopper on the window ledge. I pick it up and bring it over to the Princess. She sighs. Pika sits in silence. The grasshopper springs off my finger. I chase it around the room. The doors open, and Red walks in. Leuca follows him in. They sit in front of Pika. We all gather around and sit. I can't help but watch the grasshopper bound around the room. Red smiles and says, "Pika, well done. You've learned a lot in such a short time."

Pika opens his eyes and says, "I still have much to learn."

Red asks him, "Like I've said, you've done well. But, you know, I don't know if you're ready to fight in the battle."

Pika doesn't seem to react. The Princess would've expected Pika to be upset—at least, she's upset for him. She looks at him carefully. Pika says, "I trust you and Leuca will know when I'm ready."

Red rises and walks around Pika. She pokes him in the lower back, on the shoulder and on the knee. She even shoves him a little. She says, "I don't know if you'll ever be ready. Look at your tummy—it sticks out like a pebble in the stream, and it's soft like mud."

Pika answers, "I trust you and Leuca know best."

Red walks over to the Princess and says, "Look at your sister. She's such a spoiled child. I'm surprised you're not more like her, all selfish and …"

"Hey! Shut up!" yells the Princess. "How can you be so cruel? After all that he's done for you, after all that we've done, we could be with the unicorn now. We could be humans again. Instead, we're sitting here in this stupid tree, day after day, night after night."

Pika stands up and holds his sister. He whispers into her ear. She quiets down. Pika lets her go and walks over to Red and Leuca. Red circles him. Her red and white paws are silent. You can barely hear her tail whistling through the air. Red sticks her face in Pika's and says, "Your father deserved to die."

Pika stares back at her and says nothing. Red presses her nose against Pika's and adds, "Your mother deserved to die...even more."

Pika snaps his head, striking Red's, and he grabs her throat. He yells, "Take that back! I'll kill you!"

He suddenly hears his words echo through his head. He lets go of Red. She falls back on her feet. He looks up at the ceiling, drops his head and grimaces. He purses his lips and says, "I'm sorry Master. I lost control. I'm sorry."

Red smiles and says, "It's alright. It's good to be aware of your weaknesses."

The Princess realizes this was all a test and feels better. She relaxes and sits down on her bed. Leuca finally speaks, "Pika, tell me. Why are you here?"

Pika looks at Leuca. He answers, "To fight Moyen, and bring peace to this world."

"Why are you here? Why are you fighting our fight?"

"Because I believe in it. Moyen is evil. We have to stop him."

"Why is he evil?"

Pika replies, "Because you said so."

Leuca chuckles. "Pika, I never said that. Listen, don't hear. I'll ask you again. What do you believe? Why are you here? How did you get here?"

"We followed Naso. We heard about Moyen's ruthlessness and what's happening in Snow Forest. I've heard how the animals talk about him and are afraid of him. I believe Moyen is evil."

Leuca whispers to Red. He turns back to Pika and asks, "Pika, please spend the next two days with Red. I've asked her to take you into Snow Forest to see with your own eyes. Come back and tell me what you see and what you believe."

Pika is confused and unsure of what he did wrong. The Princess isn't sure what's happening either. She's not sure if she's joining Pika or not. Leuca stands up and quietly leaves the room. Red approaches Pika and sits down next to him. Red looks around the room, closes her eyes and quietly meditates. Several minutes pass. Pika tries to close his eyes as well, but question after question race through his mind. He thinks back through each test and tries to figure out what he did wrong. He thinks about Rhino. He wonders how he'll fight back his emotions about his mother. Red abruptly says, "Say goodbye to Annie and Naso. We'll leave after lunch and return tomorrow after dinner."

Red stands up and leaves the room. The Princess starts to get nervous. She doesn't know how she'll get through another night without her brother. She runs to him and says, "You can't go. That night you left me, I couldn't handle it. I need you here."

Pika looks at her. Surprised, she steps back. She sees something different in his eyes. She realizes he's grown. He's no longer the little brother running around the palace and making a mess of things. He's become responsible and has a focused look in his face. Pika holds her hands and says, "I'll miss you too, but I have to go. I need to find some answers. I need these answers to help me understand what I'm blind to. I'll be back. It's only one night. Naso will be here. Everyone is here. You'll be safe. I have to go."

From his look, the Princess knew she couldn't change his mind. She quietly nods.

16. ONE NIGHT

After lunch, Red and Pika leave the temple. They hike down the rocks and along the gravel trail towards Snow Forest. The Princess and I stand at the temple gates, watching them. In a few minutes, they disappear behind Mother-Child Rock, a granite precipice shaped like a mother crane standing next to her child that looms high over the temple. The Princess waits, hoping they'd turn around and come back. I look at her face. I remember seeing the most sincere sense of concern on her face.

The Princess exhales a deep breath. I ask, "Why don't you join training today? It'll take your mind off Pika."

"No, I'm not a warrior."

"Not a warrior? It's not all for fighting; it's about controlling your mind and your body. You already know a lot, and you've been training for the last few months."

"No, I'm not in the mood."

"What are you going to do when we go to battle?"

The Princess hadn't thought about it before. She only joined training to pass time and to be close to Pika. She quietly replies, "I'm not sure."

"Let's just go and see how you feel today."

* * *

Red and Pika trek down the mountain in silence. Red leads the way, and Pika follows. As they near Mercy Falls, Red stops and drinks water from the pool. Pika drinks. Red says, "When we enter the forest, we need to be careful and stay out of sight. Moyen's animals are all around. They know a rebellion is on the rise, so they are extra suspicious of any activity, especially the dholes."

Pika nods. As they quietly enter the forest and walk past the shrubs and trees, Pika looks around—he doesn't recognize the forest anymore. He hasn't been here since Master Tao dropped him and Annie off. He doesn't remember too much from that day. Now, he's more comfortable with his new body. He's learned to use his smell and other senses more keenly. They stop for a break in a small patch of aspens. They hadn't seen any other animals except for insects. Pika wonders where they all are, especially the birds.

* * *

The Princess and I walk down to the courtyard. The animals stand in line. We get in the back row. One of the teachers, a red crowned crane named Master Tzu, paces in front of us. He stops and barks out, "First position."

The Princess jumps into a slightly bent knee position with her back straight and arms out. She watches all the animals hop and turn sideways, pointing their fists forward. The teacher continues to yell out commands, and the students execute. The Princess performs the moves. After a long time, her mind tires from trying not to think about Pika, and she collapses. She lays on her back with her mouth open. I stop, lean down and hold up her head. She whispers, "Water, water. I just want some water."

She opens her eyes. She sees Master Tzu standing behind me. The crane's long beak opens, and he says, "You want some water?"

The Princess nods. He says, "Stand up. There's water by the rock cliff behind you."

She turns her head back and looks at the cliff. What is he talking about? How horrible! It's a giant slab of rock. How is she supposed to drink water? She looks at him. He smiles. She looks at me, and I shake my head in the cliff's direction.

Frustrated, the Princess lays back down. Master Tzu shakes his head and walks away. She sighs and wants to cry. How did she get here? What happened to her life? Her great life. She was the princess.

69

She had everything. Everyone listened to her. Now she can't even get a drink of water. She gets mad and frustrated. Don't these animals know who she is? She's the princess! She's someone special! She's different, she's not like everyone else. She gets more and more mad. She sits up. She looks at the cliff. She walks over to it. She's had enough of this life. The crane and all the animals turn their heads to watch. Master Tzu then orders all the students to stop watching and start practicing.

She looks up and down the rock face. There are no signs of water. It's dry as a bone. She presses her ear. To her surprise, she hears passing air. There's a hissing sound. She taps her knuckles against the rock. She hears an echo. The wall must be hollow. There may be water back there.

Knowing she can't break the rock, she looks around for a hole or some sort of opening. Just above her reach, she spots a ledge full of grass and flowers. She moves a boulder over and stands on it. After she pulls the grass out and digs out the dirt, she sticks her hand in. She feels cool damp air. She sticks her hand further in. She feels water dripping. Yes! She did it! She cups her hand and pulls out some water. She drinks it. The water tastes great. Clean, cool and refreshing. She grabs more and more out.

Master Tzu smiles. He walks over. He says, "I'm proud of you. That was quite an accomplishment. You are quite determined. You have grown." He pauses and points to the side. "But there's also a bowl of water beside the cliff."

The Princess walks over to an inset of the cliff and sees a small table with a wooden water bowl. She falls on her knees and screams, "Oh my goodness! Really?! Naso! Why didn't you tell me?"

The crane laughs and walks back to the class. Laughing hysterically, I hop over and drink some water.

The Princess asks again, "Why didn't you stop me? Why didn't you tell me it was right here?"

"You seemed so determined. I was curious," I answered.

"Curious? What if there wasn't any water behind the rock?"

"Well, it would've been entertaining. That water is so much better than this. It must've been cool and refreshing. This is a little bland and a bit warm, don't you think? Your water is fresh from the source!" I laugh.

"I can't believe this!"

* * *

Pika and Red sit in the dove tree, quiet and still. A group of dholes gathers beneath them. They yell and push one another. Other large cats and animals come in as well. A hush comes over the crowd. Pika sees a large brown pheasant walking in followed by a giant tiger. He guesses that it must be General Mantchu and Moyen. The pheasant shuffles its feet so quickly it looks like it floats across the ground. White feathers stick out underneath his beak to both sides like a mustache. His red eyes draw your stare in. He walks with dignity but just looks like a crazed and insane animal.

The tiger is three times the size of any other one, even Blue. Legend does him no justice—I know you and the other animals now fear Blue, but his grandfather was something to behold. Hypnotizing black stripes run across his burnt orange fur while old age is painted white around his eyes, cheeks and underbelly. His stark yellow eyes look like dead demons burning. Across his body, you can see scars from his many battles. Moyen walks with intention, methodically and thoughtfully. He stares ahead. You know where he's going, and you don't dare get in his way. His strong muscles radiate underneath his handsome orange, black and white fur. His grandeur is fearful yet mesmerizing and spiritual, whereas Blue is violent and malicious. They are quite different—Moyen evokes a distant and fearful respect, whereas Blue summons up feelings of contempt and disdain. With his

71

white and bluish fur with dark grey stripes, Blue may feel inadequate or something—maybe that's why he's so brutally violent.

Anyway, General Mantchu and Moyen approach and leap onto a boulder in the middle of the clearing. The pheasant says, "Time! Time! Time!"

General Mantchu shuffles back and forth, twisting his beak and staring at various animals. He screams in a high-pitched tone, "Time isn't free! Its price is heavy. The sun is high. The moon is behind. Soon the moon will fly, and the sun will die. Sniff your partner, so you can remember. And if you rejoice, it comes with a choice. Bury me if it is to be. But let us all be free!"

Pika and Red stare at one another confused. They turn their attention back to the boulder where Moyen is speaking. His voice is deep and calm, almost eerily like Leuca's. He says, "Friends, we know the time is coming when we must fight to defend what we treasure so dearly—our freedom. The rebels are looking to destroy everything we've worked to protect. We did not come this far to have it taken away. Turn to each side and look at one another. We are family. We have shed blood side by side. We have suffered at the same hands of brutality. We have eaten from the same grounds, and we have drank from the same rivers. We have watched births as we have witnessed deaths. We have loved, and we have hated. They spread lies, and now they want to fight. Brothers and sisters! I will be by your sides! As you have bled for me, I will bleed for you. It comes down to this simple little truth: They are right from their side, and we are right from ours. Let us not be mistaken. We know we are right. Tonight, we feast! In the coming days, we will bleed for freedom!"

The crowd roars with approval. The animals cheer one another, hug and throw things in the air to celebrate. Moyen and General Mantchu march off back into the forest. The animals follow after them in a long procession. After the animals are gone and the forest is silent except for the wind blowing across the long, hanging dove tree leaves, Pika and Red climb down. Red asks, "What do you think?"

"I'm confused," Pika replies. He pauses and looks at the ground. "Can I be honest?"

"Yes, of course."

"He almost sounds like Leuca. They say similar things. I'm confused. The animals here are just defending their home. Moyen wants to protect them and their freedom."

"Yes, it's a similar rhetoric. Why do you think that is?"

"I'm not sure."

"Let's head back, and you can think along the way. We'll stay overnight near Mercy Falls."

The two walk through the forest. They set up camp near Mercy Falls in a small cave. Red builds a fire, and they gather some bird eggs and bamboo leaves. Pika asks, "Everyone's right from their side, aren't they?"

Red nods.

Pika continues, "A strong person can exert his will on others, and others will follow. Most of us simply follow our emotions or the emotions of others around us."

"Drop a small pebble in a pool, and you'll see small ripples as it sinks. But those ripples disappear. Drop a large stone, and there will always be ripples."

"Is all evil relative?"

"What do you think?"

Pika replies, "If circumstances were different and I was a dhole like one I saw today, I wouldn't think Moyen was evil. I'd see things differently."

Red hands him a roasted bird egg and says, "Are we evil to eat these eggs? Am I evil since I burned them to death?"

Pika takes the egg, turns it around and sits staring at it. Red bites a hole in the shell and drinks the yolk.

* * *

Perched on the cliff, the Princess gazes at the moon. I sit beside her. She misses Pika terribly and wants to see him again. I give her a hug. She smiles. It's only the second time she's been alone without her brother. Standing up on the cliff, she looks down at the temple. Most animals have gone to bed. She sees a few candles flickering and a couple animals walking through the courtyard.

I yawn and say, "I'm going to bed now. Are you going to sleep soon?"

"I don't think I can sleep. I have to know if he's alright."

"He's fine. He's with Red."

"I know, but it's hard."

"You did good today. The training's hard, but you lasted as long as everyone."

"I don't know."

"You're tough. You'll be fine."

"Thanks."

17. THE PATH

"Pika!" The Princess screams. She runs across the courtyard to the gate and hugs her brother. He blushes in embarrassment.

"Hey sis," he says, putting one arm around her.

The Princess asks, "What kind of hug is that?"

He drops his bag and hugs her. She pushes away and looks at him. She asks, "Are you alright? Something bothering you?"

"I saw a lot. It made me think."

Red walks up and says, "Your brother learned that there are no easy answers. Nothing is as it seems. It's only the start of his journey."

The Princess is confused. I hop over and hug Pika. We all walk back into the temple and help Pika settle in. Afterwards, we head over to the rock garden, and Pika rakes the pebbles. The Princess is troubled by her brother's change. He is quiet and seems lost in his mind. She doesn't want to bother him. She walks back to her room.

During dinner, Pika remains silent and picks at his food. The Princess is unsure how to help. She and I make jokes and laugh. I whisper to her, "I can't take this silence. We need to cheer him up."

The Princess nods. I crawl under the table and make a farting sound. The Princess says, "Ewwww! Did you fart?"

Pika says, "No. Stop that."

I do it again. Then I jump out from behind and start tickling Pika. Giggling, he says, "Stop it. Stop it."

"Get out of your head. Your sister's here. She's been worried sick about you. You can't even see that."

I keep tickling him. The Princess is laughing. Pika sees her and smiles. Pika grabs me and tries to tickle me. I slip out and hop over him. He tries to catch me, but I'm too fast and nimble. I hop around making faces at him. He lunges at me, grabs my big left ear and pulls me in. He ties my tail to the leg of his chair. I yell, "Hey! Untie me!"

He laughs and unties me. The Princess says, "It's good to see you laugh."

"Yeah, it is. Sorry, I've just been thinking a lot."

"I know."

"What should we do?" he asks.

"Let's go up to the cliff. The moon's beautiful up there."

"Alright."

The three of us hike up the cliffs. The mountains' shadows loom over the trees and valleys below us as the river etches its way out to the distant sea. Red is perched meditating out on Mother-Child Rock.

At the top, I unwrap some fruit and hand them out for everyone to eat. The Princess points out the palace in the distance, "There it is, our home."

Pika says, "I barely remember it now. It feels so long ago like a bedtime story we were told."

"I know. We'll go back someday."

"I don't know if I want to go back."

She turns in surprise. "What are you saying?"

"I'm happier here," he says. He moves over next to her. "I'm doing stuff here. They appreciate me. It's different. Friendships feel real."

"I guess so, but don't you miss our stuff?"

"Not really. I had so much stuff I didn't know what to do. It didn't make me happy…having stuff that is."

"What about being human?"

"There are some stuff I miss, and other stuff I don't. Here, it's just the basics. The basic needs to live."

"I miss my bed."

"Yes! I do miss my bed." They both laugh. He hugs his sister. She feels a little sadness, but she's happy to have her brother back.

"What did you see out there?" asks the Princess.

"I came back with more questions than answers," answers Pika.

I spin around and fall on my back. They laugh. I hop up and say, "Pika, this is getting too serious. Come on…"

He ignores me and tells the Princess, "Just as we believe this is right, Moyen's army believes he is right. I never made a good Crown Prince. I never really saw one side or another. Father did. He chose a path and fought for it. Moyen, Leuca and Onensis—they all chose a path."

"You would've made a great Emperor," the Princess softly says.

"No, they all led others to believe. I can't lead others to believe if I can't lead myself. I'm a follower…like so many of us. There's nothing wrong with that. I can't see the path ahead. I need someone to find the path."

"I don't know what you're talking about."

Pika looks at the Princess and me. He says, "I can't find the path. But when someone finds a path, I do know if the path is right or wrong. And that's ok. We're all different. And I know this is the right path."

He holds his sister's hands and continues, "We're different. That's alright, Annie. You always have and always will forge your own path. Out there, under the stars, I learned more about myself in that one night than my whole life. This is the right path for me."

18. RISING MOON

Red wakes Pika and asks him to follow her. The Princess looks on in confusion. They go up to Leuca's chamber.

"Pika, I'm proud of you. You've worked hard and are dedicated. You've learned a lot. Soon, we will be going into battle. Red and I want you in our lead battalion. You'll help us defeat Moyen's army," says Leuca.

"Thank you, I'm honored. What about Annie?"

"She hasn't worked hard and isn't ready for battle."

"I know."

"She'll be a liability on the field. I think it's best for her to stay here," says Leuca.

"She won't. We stay together."

"Yes, but she'll die on the field, and it'll be a distraction for you. You can't be thinking about someone else; you can only think about yourself out there. We need you focused."

Pika is quiet and nods slowly. He says, "I understand. Can I tell her?"

"Yes, it'd be best if you did."

Pika walks back to the room. The Princess is sitting up. She can read his face that something is about to happen. She says, "No, don't tell me. I don't want to hear. You're going away, aren't you?"

Pika sits down next to her. In all their years together, this is the first time he feels like an older brother. He doesn't look at her. He looks down at the ground. He says, "We're leaving tomorrow evening. I'm joining Leuca and Red. It'd be best for you to stay here. I don't want anything to happen to you."

The Princess stands up. "What about you? I don't want anything to happen to you." She paces the room and continues, "No, no, no. You're my little brother. You have to listen to what I say. You have to stay. You can't go. If you go, we go together. We stay together. We're all we have!"

Pika looks up at her, and tears start to roll down. "I'm sorry sis. I have to fight. It's my calling. You can't come—I don't want anything to happen to you."

"I'm coming!"

"You don't know how to fight. You'll die out there."

"You're going to die. What then? I'm supposed to stay here and just wait for the news? No, if you go, I'm going. You can't stop me!"

Pika grabs her by the shoulders and says, "You have to stay here. I can't focus and fight if you're out there. It'll distract me. I'll just be looking out for you."

She stares him in the eyes. They grab one another and hug. They start to cry. The Princess knows she can't survive the battle, and she knows she can't stop her brother. Her heart is torn, and the tears pour out of her like water off a waterfall. She grabs the fur on his neck tight. She doesn't want to let go. She already lost her parents, and she can't lose him. The pain is hurting her. He pulls her off and looks at her.

He touches his forehead to hers and says, "Annie, it'll be okay.

You've seen me train and fight. You know I'm one of the best. I'll be fine. I'll be back, and we'll continue onto the unicorn."

She nods, but she doesn't believe his words.

The rest of the morning and afternoon, the Princess is full of sadness, and the minutes pass slowly as she tries to remember every moment, every movement, and every sound of his voice. She doesn't want to forget. She already knows she's forgotten most of her mother and father. She doesn't want to forget him.

Pika spends the morning practicing his routines and exercises. Leuca and Red gather Pika and the other leaders to review the attack and defense strategies. They look over the battle field and discuss how they'll escape if need be, and how they'll attack Moyen's troops.

In the early evening, Red calls all the animals into the courtyard. She gathers them all for one last meal together. Leuca walks in. He says, "I won't lie. We all know some of us will not return. Some of our loved ones, some of our friends, some of our acquaintances will remain on the battle field. I ask us all to be present in this moment. Let us now enjoy this meal together. Enjoy our time together. Hug one another. Kiss one another. Let your mind not wonder about things unknown. Let your mind be present. That is where we'll find our strength and our peace tonight."

Dinner is quiet. Everyone tries to focus on the time they have together, but they all are thinking about the upcoming war. The Princess, Pika and myself eat together. I tell jokes and keep the conversation light, but it's difficult. The Princess and Pika aren't sure what to talk about. She tells Pika to be careful, and he tells her the same.

After dinner, we walk up to the top of the cliffs to watch the moon rise. I leave the two of them alone. The Princess and Pika sit on the edge of the cliff. They look out at the valley below. They talk about their old palace and reminisce about their childhood. They laugh about different tricks they played on people, and they talk about their mother and father.

The Princess looks at Pika and suddenly remembers hearing her father being killed. The sounds of screaming and swords piercing skin sends chills through her. She doesn't want Pika to die. She can't get rid of the sounds in her head. She gazes up at the night sky. She finds a familiar star. A long deep breath helps her calm down a little bit. It's different this time. Pika isn't tied up like her father. He's a great fighter, and he'll do fine. Leuca and Red will be there. It's different this time, she tells herself. She takes another deep breath and exhales. The Princess hugs Pika and says, "I love you, Pika. Come back safe."

"I will. Stay safe. I love you, Annie."

"Mother would be proud of you."

19. WAR

As Leuca leads the army out of the temple, the Princess and I make our way up the cliff—it provides the best vantage point. She watches the army wind its way along the rocky mountain trail from Mother-Child Rock past Nine Dragon Waterfall and down towards the base of Cloud Mountain. Their torches and candles make them look like a glowing caterpillar slinking along a path. She can't see Pika, but she knows he's in the front somewhere along Leuca's side.

The Princess' heart is beating fast. Her hands are shaking. She can't stand the wait. I tell her some jokes. She can't take her mind off her brother. Anxiety begins to consume her, and she starts breathing fast and trembling. She tries to think about other things. She looks at the sky and the trees and the rocks on the ground, but her mind thinks about her father, General Sun and Pika dying, and she keeps wiping the tears from her eyes. I tell her a joke about a blind mouse who has to find his way out of a cheese maze. She grabs me by the shoulders and says, "Stop Naso! It's not helping. I need to go!"

"What are you talking about?"

"I can't stay here."

"Princess, you'll die. You can't fight."

"I'm not planning to fight. I'll stay in the distance and watch."

"That's even worse. You don't want to helplessly watch while animals die."

"I can't just stay here and do nothing."

I see she's determined, and I decide it's better to stick together. I tell her, "Ok, I'll go with you."

The Princess smiles and says, "Thank you."

We make our way back down the cliffs to our room. We pack food and candles. We run out of the temple to catch up with the army, but we keep our distance so we won't be seen.

The fall sky is dark. A slight wind sweeps across and soothes the animals. The army spends the night walking down the treacherous dark trail to Snow Forest. At Mercy Fall, they stop to rest and eat. Leuca reviews the strategy with his leaders. They break into four groups. Pika stays with Leuca. Red leads a large contingent down south.

Digging in, each of the groups waits quietly. They've surrounded Moyen's army who are sleeping in the clearing in the middle of the forest. There are several hundred dholes, tigers, mountain lions and leopards. In the nearby trees, hundreds of hawks and eagles rest. They have all come in to prepare and to fight with Moyen. Some monkeys and birds patrol in the trees, but they are sleepy and fall in and out of sleep. They don't notice Leuca's army moving in.

Leuca's army of bears, pandas, monkeys, gibbons, cranes and wolverines stand at four stations—north, south, east and west. Leuca and Pika are positioned at the north side with a hundred troops. They quietly gesture to the different animals to move around and get positioned. The animals take turns resting and napping. The plan is for everyone to wait until dawn. Leuca, Pika and Red will enter the clearing, and talk to Moyen. Leuca wants to see if a peaceful agreement can be reached. He doesn't want any bloodshed.

The Princess and I make our way down to Mercy Falls. We see the animals in the distance. I gesture to the Princess to keep quiet. Because I don't want us to be seen, we enter the forest and head up northeast towards the edge. We quietly run behind the trees and shrubs until we find a large dove tree. We scramble up the trunk and find a long, smooth branch that reaches out across the forest. From on top of a giant leaf, we rest and hide as the slight wind sways us back and forth. We see Moyen and his army resting in the clearing, and we make out the shadows of Leuca and Pika just west of us. We can see how everyone's arranged themselves.

As the rosy fingers of dawn creep over the horizon and reach down into the forest and its clearing, Leuca signals to Pika it's time to go. Red sees Leuca walking in and joins. The three of them approach an awake and waiting Moyen with General Mantchu. Moyen calmly says, "Welcome Leuca, I never expected you to come down here ready to wage war."

Leuca says, "There doesn't need to be war. We should discuss this. From one aging spirit to another, we've seen enough killing in our lives. Let's not bear witness to more."

"So Onensis has sent you to do his dirty deed? Coward. He always hides behind others. What's he going to do? If you prove victorious, he'll come and take credit. Where will you go then? Back to the mountains to eat bamboo?"

"Moyen, don't change the topic. We, like you and your supporters, just want peace. I want to talk to you about how we can all co-exist and not fight."

"All good words, Leuca. All good words," Moyen says. He jumps off his boulder and approaches Leuca. He presses his face into Leuca's. Pika stands by. Red motions him to relax. Moyen continues, "Leuca, this isn't about 'talk' and 'peace'. It's about trust. Neither side trusts the other. Even if I promised peace and equality, Onensis wouldn't believe me. One night, he'd send someone to assassinate me. On the other hand, if I give in and Onensis rules, I'd never sleep. I'd lay awake every night wondering when Onensis would take it all away. So you see, Leuca, the problem is deep. That's why violence is such a sweet, sweet way of solving it. By nightfall, one of us will be standing, and all will be resolved. Peace will live in this forest again."

"Moyen, those are lies you've told yourself and others."

"Then where is Onensis? Why does he not stand with his own? He has to convince you—the one spirit we all hold in deep respect— to come and fight his battle."

"He doesn't need to convince me. I've seen your ways."

"Leuca, you know I've always have respected you."

"This, I know."

"Then hear me. This is not your fight. I have nothing but respect for you. You have lived the life all spirits should honor and follow. Do not tarnish your legacy."

Leuca quietly stares at Moyen. Both generals, Red and Mantchu, remain silent. Pika stands close to Leuca. Moyen looks at Pika and says, "What is this? A human? You've brought a human to the fight?"

Leuca replies, "He's no longer a human."

"A human will always be a human."

"Look at him, he's not a human. He's a rabbit."

"Anyway, take him back to your army, and we'll settle this."

"Moyen, we can all live peacefully together. We can co-exist, all in freedom."

"When Onensis shows his face, I'll believe you. Leuca, I don't want to kill you, but I will. I want you to know this. You know you are not a warrior. This is not your war. I don't want to kill you. I'll only say this once more. Elder Spirit, I have nothing but the highest respect for you and for all that you stand for."

"Then listen to me, and let's resolve this."

Moyen turns his back and leaps up onto his boulder. He glares at Red, Pika and Leuca, and snarls, "When you are ready, we fight."

Leuca looks at Red and Pika, motioning for them to leave. They each march back to their stations.

There is no wind. The morning sun rests just above the trees, and the leaves are still golden from the morning glow. The grass looks like a carpet of gold. The entire forest is silent. From across the meadow, Leuca and Moyen stare at one another, waiting for the other to make the first move. Leuca knows he has to make it; Moyen is defending and doesn't have to do anything. Leuca closes his eyes and takes a deep breath through his nostrils. He exhales. He yells, "Rebels! Onward we fight!"

The rebels storm the clearing. It's a trap. Many of them fall into pits covered with leaves and branches. They howl in pain as they fall onto sharpened stakes. Pika is horrified. He's never watched animals die in front of his eyes before. He's paralyzed. He can't move. Leuca notices. He runs back—for a large panda, he's very agile and nimble. He shakes Pika. "Pika, snap out of it! You have to focus. Or you'll get killed. Move!"

Pika shakes his head. He looks for Mantchu. He can't find him. A spotted leopard leaps onto him. Pika tries to shake him off, but the leopard is too big. The leopard tries to bite his face. Pika moves. He slips out of the leopard's grasp. With a swing of his sword, he cuts off the leopard's tail. The leopard wails in pain. Pika then clambers onto the leopard's back and stabs him. The leopard collapses. Blood seeps and then streams out of his chest. The dark crimson fluid stains the grass. Pika falls off. He watches the leopard's eyes slowly fade, rolling back until only the whites of his eyes remain. Pika's never killed anyone before. He's stunned again. It doesn't feel real. His hands feel numb, and the sword drops to the grass. A tingling sensation runs up his legs through his spine and into the tips of his ears. He snaps himself out of it and grabs his sword. He focuses and charges another leopard.

The rebels maneuver past the traps and start fighting Moyen's army. The animals clash with weapons as well as bare paws. From our spot, the Princess and I watch the carnage. The animals kill and wound one another. We can't see which side is winning. The Princess is traumatized. I am as well. We both want to throw up. We're sick to our stomachs. I want to leave, but I know she wants to stay here with Pika. At some point, neither one of us can watch anymore. We shield our eyes and wait. The sound of death surrounds us, and we can't escape.

Not even my humor and my joy in life can bring any light to this situation. Osani, this day changed me. Witnessing all that bloodshed and all those deaths shattered my faith and hope in this world. Nothing I could say or think would bring back those lives—many, many friends died that day. Nothing could piece my broken faith together. On this day, I lost my youth.

Throughout the morning and into the afternoon, Moyen's army slowly makes more and more progress. The rebels lose ground and fall back to the forest to regroup. Their attacks continue to fail as Moyen's army introduces more and more treacherous traps and weapons. They fire a catapult of fire into the south side to chase out the rebels who then run straight into a giant venomous snake pit. Moyen easily kills all the rebels who get in his way. He is too big, too agile and too ruthless to be stopped. Small bands of mountain lions continue to come after Red and Leuca. The two of them can't find a moment to break free and to regroup.

By evening, the toll of death rises and rises until the battle comes down to a few dozen animals. The Princess and I move closer to the clearing. We see Moyen and Leuca move towards the center and stare at one another. They circle one another like a dance. The other animals stand back and watch. Moyen charges. He slides in low against Leuca's legs, flipping him over. He crushes Leuca's throat with his tail. Then he digs his claws into Leuca's shoulders and pulls the claws down his biceps. The blood oozes out of Leuca's arms. Leuca grabs Moyen and throws him against the boulder. He rams him with all his weight, breaking a couple ribs. Moyen falls to the ground, holding his chest. Pika thinks, "Attack, Leuca, attack. This is your chance."

But Leuca doesn't. He stands over Moyen and says, "Let's end this. We needn't kill one another."

Moyen glares up at Leuca, smiles and then punches his claws into Leuca's chest. He pulls out his claws holding Leuca's heart. The blood drips off his claws. A piercing howl passes over the forest. The life in Leuca immediately escapes from him. His eyes look up to the heavens and then roll back. His body is lifeless and collapses to the ground like an old hollow fir tree collapsing in a forest. Moyen places Leuca's heart on his lifeless body and kowtows in a moment of silence. A streak of fire burns in the evening sky as if a galloping unicorn had just blazed across. Red and Pika scream, "Noooo!"

Moyen smirks, "It's over."

Pika charges in. The Princess screams and almost falls out of the tree, "No!"

Pika stands in front of Moyen and confronts him. Moyen just laughs, "Be gone, you tiny human bunny. You don't stand a chance. I'd crush you with a finger, and I'd enjoy every second of it. I'd love to kill a spirit and a human all on the same day."

"Then do it!" Pika yells defiantly.

Moyen scowls at him. "Your last chance. Go away."

Pika leaps up and jumps off Moyen's nose to pull out his whiskers. Moyen growls. He swings at Pika. Pika is acrobatic and vaults over Moyen's attacks. He continues to strike and frustrate Moyen.

Moyen roars. He swings his right claw as Pika is leaping at him. Moyen slices Pika across the shoulder and chest. Pika falls to the ground. Moyen smashes his tail across Pika's head. Pika lays motionless with blood oozing out of his lacerated chest. The Princess screams, scrambles down the tree and races to him along with Red and me.

Moyen stands on his boulder and yells, "It's over! You all belong to me!"

20. AWAKENINGS

Pika opens his eyes. Everything is blurry. Unable to sit up, he opens his mouth, but no words come out. His neck has a sharp, piercing pain. Blinking his eyes rapidly, the room finally comes into focus. He looks around the empty room, seeing shelves of various bowls full of leaves, nuts and herbs. He realizes he's in some sort of hospital room. He stares at the tree branch ceiling.

The door opens. Annie walks in. She runs over and hugs Pika. "You're awake! I'm so happy!" she screams.

Red and I run in, hearing Annie's voice. We all surround Pika. Red says, "You're a tough rabbit. You had us all scared, especially your sister. You're lucky to have someone who loves you that much."

Pika looks at his sister. He tries to talk, but no sound comes out. She realizes what he's doing and says, "Don't worry. Save your energy. You still have a long way to recover. Moyen seriously hurt you. The good news is that you're awake."

I hop up onto the bed and give him a kiss on the cheek. Red says, "Rest up, we have everything else taken care of. When you're better, we'll take you outside. For now, just stay here and rest."

Pika nods. Annie hugs him again. The three of us walk out. He hears us talking, but he can't make out what we are saying. He realizes something horrible has happened. He wonders if he'll ever walk and talk again.

Outside, Annie starts crying. Red gently pats her back and comforts her. "Don't worry, Annie. He's awake now. We don't have to tell him for a long time. You must stay strong. Moyen can't find out he's awake. We have to protect him."

Annie nods and wipes the tears away. She looks up and around. She wonders how we all got to this point. We now live in a prisoner camp in Snow Forest. Winter has set in—snow covers the ground except for a patch where the animals are desperately farming in frozen dirt. Icicles hang off tree branches and the camp huts. In every direction, she can see the wooden barrier wall built thirty cranes high. All around, Moyen's soldiers stand, watching over us. The occasional bird flying overhead reminds her that there is another world out there and makes her determined to find a way out.

Near the walls, the rebel animals farm patches of vegetables for Moyen's kingdom. They till the ground. They plant and pick vegetables. All the animals are skin and bones. They are freezing, they are malnourished, and they are desperate. Away from the wall, other animals are busy building twig furniture and sewing leaf blankets. The constant watch of soldiers makes their lives miserable—no one can speak, no one can stand up and stretch, and no one can socialize. Although everyone can see one another, they feel alone and isolated.

Over the past few months, Annie earned the other animals' respect, not because she demanded it or even wanted it, but because she worked hard every day to keep everyone's spirits up, and they saw her taking care of Pika. After the battle, she was broken—her ambitions to find the unicorn, to transform herself back to a human, and to relive her old life all disappeared. She focused on healing Pika and helping the other animals—she tried to be an example of how to live in this difficult situation.

With Pika's coma, he required constant care. Every morning, she was the first to wake, and she snuck over to check on him. In the hospital ward, she grew close to the other animals and helped them get better. Most of them lost their loved ones in the war and didn't have anyone to care for them. Admiration and respect for her dedication to the wounded grew and grew. After a while, Red started to come by everyday to help Annie. During breaks, Annie asked Red to teach her martial arts. Her sessions grew longer and longer. Often, she asked me to join, but I couldn't keep up with her and just ended up watching. I don't think she ever knew why she was doing this, but it was her escape. These two things helped get her mind off our terrible situation.

Each evening, the soldiers marched us all back to long dining halls where we ate boiled rice. Annie knew we were all just dying a slow death. She ate half her bowl and saved the rest to bring to Pika. Every night, through an underground tunnel, Annie slipped in to feed him her rice. She also brought him water.

Now, as she looks across the fields, she doesn't know if she's happy he's awake or if she's more sad. She just knows this isn't a way to live. Her mind wanders and thinks about this for the first time in a while. She'd been so focused on helping her brother, she never thought about her own situation. Now, he's awake, and she's thinking about the future. She knows this isn't right. She knows they can't survive here. Moyen will work them until they all die. Then he'll replace them all with new prisoners.

Annie asks Red, "If we never attacked Moyen, would we still be in the temple? Would Leuca still be alive?"

Red looks at the sky and replies, "Annie, never think about 'what if'. You'll never find peace in that question. Rather, we have to learn from the past to create a world that isn't 'what if' but 'what is'."

"It's tough. Pika's awake now. It got me thinking. I don't know… Actually, I do know. We can't live here. We can't die here. This isn't living."

"You probably haven't seen how you've changed, Annie."

"What do you mean?"

"What do you think I mean?"

"I don't know. I'm weaker. I'm skinnier. I'm hungry and thirsty all the time."

Red smiles and decides to keep quiet—she doesn't want to influence Annie's change. Red replies, "Yes, we all are. It's not going to last."

Annie looks into the distance. She still thinks about 'what if' this never all happened. What if she never went to the village and hurt the witch's son? What if she treated the palace workers better? What if she listened to her father? What if she listened to her mother, instead of forgetting her and being angry at her for dying? She starts to cry. Her mother. She hadn't thought about her in so long. Her father always said to learn from her mother. Annie never wanted to. She thought her mother was weak. She wanted to be like her father. But the people loved her mother.

Her mother, Empress Sophie, was tall, lean and beautiful. Her long, soft, silken hair flowed down her shoulders and back like moonlight across a cliff. She had an apricot-shaped face and large eyes. People often said Annie looked like her mother. She walked gracefully and spoke gently but strong. She was a doctor's daughter.

Annie learned after her death that she was forced to marry her father—rather, the Emperor forced her to marry him. The Emperor was riding through town one day and saw Sophie hiding behind her parents. He ordered them to move forward. He asked Sophie's father for her hand in marriage. Her father knew he couldn't say 'no'. Sophie also knew she had no choice. The town knew too.

In the beginning of their marriage, Sophie would ride her horse through town every morning. She would provide food to children and elderly people. She would stop and talk to people, especially her friends and family. Her father was a respected doctor. When the Emperor came with her, the towns people would look angrily at him and not talk to him. Over time, he grew annoyed and told her not to visit town. With General Sun's help, she still would sneak out. When the Emperor found out, he locked Sophie in her room until she promised never to go back.

The palace workers told the townspeople and her parents about this. Her father visited the palace and asked to speak with Sophie. He told her to relent to the Emperor's request—it served no one any good for her to be locked away. He didn't want Sophie to die alone. They all agreed that Sophie wouldn't leave, but her family would visit every morning.

After Annie and Pika were born, Sophie found joy in raising her children. She took great care of her children. Pika was especially close to Sophie. As Annie grew older, she looked up to her father more. Sophie saw this and was saddened. She tried to teach Annie about respecting and caring for others. Annie wouldn't listen. She liked to be powerful and in control. Her mother always said, "True power comes from respect, not from ruthlessness."

Annie never understood until now. When her mother grew ill, Annie thought it was a sign of weakness. Her father said her mother was sick, but she overheard the palace staff gossip. They said she tried to drown herself in the well, and General Sun found her and cared for her. Either way, she found all of it to be a sign of weakness.

Sophie's family and Pika spent a lot of time with her in her final days. Annie, on the other hand, avoided her. Sophie would ask to see Annie, but Annie refused. She would ride her horse in the fields or run around the palace screaming at the workers. The Emperor told Annie to spend time with her mother—even he respected her. Annie still refused.

One night, the Emperor came in and said, "Annie, your mother is dying. You must see her and spend all the time you can with her."

"She's just weak, Emperor."

He became enraged and yelled, "Never say that! Your mother is not weak! She's the woman that I love and the woman who holds the most power in this kingdom. I may rule this kingdom, but she makes it worth living in."

Annie was surprised but still stubborn. She just moved to the corner of her room and played with a toy. The Emperor approached her and said, "Everyone respects your mother, and she's held in high respect. People are afraid of me—that is never how you should rule the kingdom should that time come."

Annie shook her head, stood up and said, "I want to be like you. You're strong. You're feared. I want everyone to be scared of me."

The Emperor grabbed her shoulders and stared at her. "Look! Your mother is dying! How can you be so cold-hearted? How could we have such an ungrateful child?"

Annie pulled away. The Emperor stormed out and slammed the door. Her mother died three days later without Annie ever coming by. For a week, the entire kingdom mourned her loss. People came from all around the kingdom to attend her funeral. A trail of white and yellow orchids stretched from her childhood home to the palace. On the third night, the villagers spoke about a unicorn galloping across the clouds at night on flames, and legend grew that Empress Sophie had turned into a unicorn spirit.

After her death, the mood at the palace changed. The Emperor wasn't the same. He was constantly full of sorrow. Pika also grew more hostile. Before, he was gentle and loving. Now, he didn't know how to behave. Her family continued to come to see Pika, but after time, Pika's behavior grew intolerable, and they stopped. The Emperor and his children soon grew cold and isolated. No one talked to one another, and everyone did their own activities. Without Sophie, the palace became cold and lonely.

Annie wipes her eyes. Red is right. Pika is awake. She has to move forward.

21. DOWN BUT NOT OUT

As spring draws near and the snow has melted, the mood of the prisoners picks up. They hear birds migrating back and singing. Their fur are slowly getting a healthy glow back. Grass and flower buds emerge out of the cold earth. Pika is able to speak now and hobble around the hospital ward. With no real food, however, Red, myself and everyone continue to grow weaker. This morning, we wake up early and walk around the camp. Red looks out at the fields and says, "We survived the winter. With spring, they'll just work us harder until we all die."

Annie says, "That's Moyen's plan."

Red nods. A silence falls among us. Annie stares at the treetops dancing in the wind. She closes her eyes and listens to the wind sweeping across the trees and fields—she imagines she's a swallow following the wind up and down the valleys across grass tops and through puffs of clouds. She opens her eyes and sees a couple of young golden monkeys with their blue noses covered with long golden brown hair picking up broken branches. She wonders what they're doing and follows them back to the dining hall. Just outside the door by the porch steps, they laugh and chat while building two small huts and a bridge that goes from one to the other. Annie smiles. In this terrible situation, these children remain children. How can she learn from them?

Annie remembers her childhood and running around the palace. It seems that's all she does now. She spends a lot of her time reminiscing about her childhood and her family. She doesn't really have anything else to think about. She has no future to look forward to, and she doesn't want to dwell on the present and the misery they all face. She'd rather find warmth and joy in her memories. Emptying her mind, she feels the warm morning sun on her cheeks and the wind blowing through her short rabbit hair.

Annie looks around and whispers, "Red, isn't there anything we can do?"

Red opens her eyes and says, "What? I didn't hear you."

"Can't we get out of here?"

"I'm sure a few of us can escape, but I can't leave everyone here."

"We can't stay here anymore."

Annie looks at me and thinks about how we met. She grabs me and asks, "Naso! Remember the unicorn?"

I shake my head.

"Remember, we were after the unicorn."

"Oh, yes, that was a long time ago."

"Do you think it's true?"

"What?"

"The unicorn grants wishes."

"I don't know. That's what they say." I look at Red for a sign. Red looks deep in thought.

Annie asks her, "Red, Red. Do you believe in the unicorn?"

Red thinks about the question and replies, "I don't know. I'm not one to believe in superstitions and myths—I believe in what my eyes see."

She pauses and then adds, "But when I was very young, a friend of my grandmother found the unicorn and was cured of her illness. She was determined in searching out Qilin."

"Is that its name? Did she ask for eternal life?"

"Ha ha, no. She wanted to—everyone does. When she found Qilin, she couldn't do it. She felt selfish. Instead, she asked for her illness to be cured. Qilin looked at her and touched her with her long, spiraling antlers. My grandmother's friend fell asleep. When she awoke, she was cured. She came home and told everyone. I remember seeing her healthy and vibrant."

"Does that mean you believe?"

"It means I know nothing."

The guards are walking through the living quarters and waking up the animals. They are yelling, "Wake up! Time to work!"

The three of us return to our hut to prepare for the day. We head out to the fields. In the grueling sun, our bent backs ache and throb. We yank and pull crops out of the dry dusty dirt. Throughout the day, Pika peeks out of the hospital ward hut to see the animals in the fields. He's disgusted he can't help. It's torture sitting in the hut with nothing to do and unable to assist. Each week, one or two animals pass out working in the fields. The guards prevent us from helping. The animals are left to die. We then have to carry the dead and bury them that night. Everyday is sad and emotional. We all know it's just a matter of time. Every evening, when we eat, we all wonder when it will end. But we keep going. It's not in our nature to quit.

As I'm tilling the soil, I hear an animal collapse near me. I turn around. Annie's on the ground. I want to run to her and help, but I can't. She's limp and lifeless like a mound of mud. She has no energy. Her face is in the dirt. She can barely breathe. She turns her face. The dirt and rocks scrape her cheek. She opens her eyes and sees Red and me in the distance looking at her with worry. She spits the dirt out of her mouth. She closes her eyes and feels the warm sun, the hard dirt, and the sweat rolling off her body. She can't die this way. This isn't who she is. She isn't going to die a prisoner. She isn't going to die wrongfully. Rage and determination start to boil within her. She wasn't born into this world to leave this way. No, not this way. She disrespected her mother. She disrespected her father. But she's learned. Yes, she has. She stood by her brother. And now, she will stand by her friends. She's not going to let Moyen beat her. She opens her eyes and pushes herself up with all her might. She sits up on her knees. I'm relieved. I smile. She looks at Red and me. We both see a different look in her. She looks purposeful and angry. I don't know what to make of it. She stands on one knee, and then she stands up straight. The guards approach her just in case she does something.

Annie returns to her field work, but she works harder and harder. I don't understand. As the evening sun sets, the guards move all of us back to the dining hall. We line up to get our food. Annie gets her bowl of rice. She follows her usual practice of eating half of it and saving the rest for her brother. During dinner, I ask if she's alright. She nods. Then she says, "I'll find the unicorn."

"What are you talking about?"

"I'm going to escape tonight and find the unicorn. We can't die here. I won't let it happen. I'll get us out. This is no way for us to live and to die."

Red and I are shocked and stare at one another. I don't know what to say. Red says, "Annie, I've never said this because I don't think you're aware, and I don't want to ruin the purity of what you've done. But we need you. You've carried us these past few months. You've cared for the injured, stood by the weak and given us hope. You've helped our lives. You've shown us how to get water out of the ground. You've shown us how to make shelter and beds. You've taught us much. I've had my moments of doubt, but I come back to you and your change. Every morning, I wait for you and see what new hope you bring. You can't leave—if anything happens to you, I'm not sure what will happen to us."

Annie hugs Red and says, "You're too kind, Red. I've done nothing. I've learned everything from you, Naso, Pika and Leuca. I've been a horrible person all these years. I know that now. It's time for me to make up for my past. I have to find the unicorn. It's our only way out. We don't have the strength nor the numbers to win another war."

Red says, "Annie, let's consider the consequences."

"I've thought about it. Nothing will change my mind," she says. She looks at us and asks, "Please take care of Pika. I'll tell him tonight. Take care of him. I'll be back."

I ask, "What are you going to ask the unicorn?"

"To save us."

"How?"

"Turn Pika and me back to humans. I'll find people to come and rescue us."

Red says, "I don't know if that's the answer."

"Why?"

"Humans don't care about us. You won't either. You may not remember us."

"Red, we can't live this way. I just want to go back to the old times."

"When? When you were human?"

"Yes. Or when we were in the temple. Or when we were children. I don't know. Just anywhere but here."

Red holds her and says, "Just be patient. We can survive."

"Red, you know as well as me that Moyen will work us to death. There is no escape. I have to do something. I can't sit around waiting to die. I can't watch Pika die. I can't watch you and Naso die."

For once, I'm speechless. I don't know what to say. Red doesn't either. We just look at one another. We know she is stubborn, and once she makes up her mind, she won't change it. She hugs us.

Annie returns to our hut and sneaks through the tunnel to the hospital ward. She gives Pika the bowl of rice. While he's eating, she says, "Pika, do you remember the unicorn?"

He nods his head as he chews.

She continues, "I'm going to go find her."

He stops eating and looks at her. "What? Are you joking?"

"No, don't try to stop me. We have to escape."

"And your solution is to find the unicorn? Why don't we just try to escape?"

"You're too weak. And I'm not going to leave behind all of our friends. The only way is to find the unicorn and ask for our release."

"I'm coming with you."

"No, you're not. You're too weak. You'll die out there. I'm going by myself."

"You're not going!"

"Shhhh, stop yelling. They'll know you're awake." She covers his mouth.

He pulls her hand away and whispers, "Annie, you can't go. You're all I have in this world."

"Red and Naso will take care of you. I'll be back. I'm the only one who can do this." She looks at him and hugs him. She says, "You know this is true. It's in our nature. I let you go fight. Now, let me go."

Pika closes his eyes and is quiet for a long time. He hugs her back and holds her tight. He says, "I love you. Come back."

She nods.

"When will you leave?"

"Tonight. I don't want to think about it too long, otherwise, I may not do it."

22. ESCAPE

Annie stops to rest. Sweat rolls down her face. She wipes it off on her forearm. The tunnel is dark and cold. The dirt is damp this far under the surface. Bugs crawl around. The air is humid. It's difficult to breathe, and it takes a lot of energy to catch her breath. Her eyes have adjusted to the darkness. She continues to dig. Over the past few months, she's learned to get a good sense of direction. She knows she has to dig far enough away from the prison camp that she won't be seen. She is tired. She sits down. She looks at her hands and feet. They're covered in calluses and dirt. She tries to lick them clean. Then she realizes how far she's come. She's definitely turning into a rabbit— half a year ago, she wouldn't have dare lick her hands.

After a few more hours of digging, Annie decides she's far out enough. She puts her hands above her head and starts burrowing towards the surface. In time, she's back at the surface. The moon is high and casts a brilliant cyan glow across the trees and fields. She looks around, and nothing looks familiar. She must be out. She runs towards the nearest boulders she sees.

Perched atop a giant boulder, she looks out. She sees the camp faraway. It's at least a few hours journey. She feels comfortable. She stands up. She looks around to scout her location. She recognizes the distant tree line near Mercy Falls. She must be on the other end of Snow Forest. She'll need to secretly travel through Snow Forest to get to Cloud Mountain. Then she'll need to find the desert on the other side. She doesn't have nocturnal instincts, so she decides to eat some plants and sleep.

The rising sun wakes her up. She rubs her eyes. She leaps back. "Moyen!" she screams.

Moyen smirks and stares at her. He says, "What guts. What determination. I admire that. Don't worry, I won't harm you. If I wanted to, I would've killed you in your sleep."

She scoots up against a boulder and sees that she's encircled by Moyen's army, including General Mantchu. She says, "Leave me alone. What do you want? I haven't done anything wrong."

General Mantchu approaches and says, "Stupid, stupid, stupid! You must think of us that way. You belong in the camp. Or way, way, way down in the earth. But not in a tunnel."

"I don't know what you're talking about. What camp? I live here in Snow Forest."

"Stupid! You human," snarled General Mantchu. The brown pheasant leans into her and glares into her eyes. The General's red eyes burn into Annie's brain. She's nervous but stands her ground.

100

"Don't worry about him," Moyen says. He walks up and nudges General Mantchu aside. "I'm quite impressed. From a spoiled human princess to a hopeless rabbit to a spiritual leader, I'm quite impressed."

"What are you talking about?"

Moyen laughs and says, "Ha! You are naive. You don't realize the influence you have, do you?"

"What? I'm not following."

"The prisoners all look up to you, including Red. I've been watching. You give them hope. You showed them the way by making their lives easier and pushing them forward. Without you there, they are defeated. But with you…they have…hope."

"I don't believe you. You're a liar."

"You just need to open your eyes."

"What do you want with me?"

"What do I want?" laughs Moyen. He is silent and then smiles. "I want you."

"What?" says Annie, and she gives a confused look.

"I want you to be my empress. Together, we'll rule this forest in peace."

"No!" Annie screams. She tries to run away, but a dhole grabs her.

Moyen pulls her into him. He whispers, "Annie, I've fallen for you. I love you. Together, we'll bring peace. My kingdom with your animals, it's perfect."

"No, you don't love me. You don't know me! You're just using me."

"Now, now. You're just upset. I do love you. I've watched you all these months. I've grown quite fond of you. I want to learn all you know. I want to…"

"Stop right there! You're a horrible liar."

Moyen chuckles. "You don't know me. You just need some time to get to know me."

"I'll never believe you, and I'll never love you. You killed Leuca."

He laughs and lets her go. "I suppose you're right. But you can't deny it's admirable. It's up to you. You be my empress, and you save your friends—they'll all be released. You don't, and well, you all will die. It's up to you. I wouldn't want all those deaths on me."

Annie's face turns white, and she realizes she has no real choice. She remembers her mother. She falls to her knees and cries. Moyen motions for his army to move back as he backs away. He sits, cleans his whiskers and lets her consider her options. Annie rubs her eyes, but it's no use. She can't stop crying—she was full of hope to find the unicorn, and now she faces life with a monster. With no choice but to marry him, her life as a prisoner flashes before her eyes. She reminds herself that Pika, Red, Naso and everyone else will be free to live. It's what she wants for them. Her heart is so heavy. She can't stand up. She lays on the ground, crying.

Annie cries for her life. She cries for the loss of all hope. She cries for no escape. She cries for her mother.

23. THE EMPRESS RETURNS

Under the early afternoon sun, Annie walks with Moyen into camp. The gate opens. Although she'd only been gone the night, she sees all of us differently. We are bone thin. She looks down at her feet and the ground; she can't bring herself to look at anyone. She feels ashamed and disgraced. She can feel our gazes on her. Moyen pushes her in. They walk towards the plaza where a small circle of flowers grows. Annie planted this the first day and told everyone there would be hope as long as these flowers lived.

Moyen declares, "Friends, welcome Annie back. We are here to celebrate wonderful news."

A murmur goes across the crowd as they wonder what Moyen's talking about. He continues, "Over the past several months, I've been watching one of yours and have fallen madly in love. She has captured my mind and my heart. Annie, your Annie, will become my empress. Together, we'll rule this world. She will be your empress as I'm your emperor."

The crowd is silent. Everyone is shocked. No one knows what to do or say. They all look at Annie for some response. They want her to say it's a joke. She hangs her head. She can't bear to look at anyone.

"When we wed, you will all be freed. We will live in peace. As I know Annie loves you all and has secured your freedom, I know you will all do what is right," says Moyen. He kisses Annie on the cheek and nudges her to speak.

She quietly speaks, "My friends, don't despair. I will be fine. You will all be freed and be able to live as you did before. I will live to ensure you all will have a better life."

One by one, the animals all stand up and bow their heads towards Annie. Tears come down their faces as they all hold hands. Annie is moved and straightens up. She feels the love of the animals and knows she's doing what's best for them. As she looks out, she sees Pika in the back. He's leaning on Red. He nods to her. She nods back. She fights back her tears.

She sees me crying. I wave a little bit but go back to wiping my eyes—I can't stop crying. She gives me a little smile. I know what she's thinking, and I try to stand up brave and courageous. She doesn't need me to make her situation worse. She needs me to be strong.

Moyen sees Red and Pika, and whispers to General Mantchu to get them. Annie looks around the crowd. She hears commotion and sees the guards taking Pika and Red. She looks at Moyen who just smiles at her. He says, "Insurance."

"Let them go!"

"I'm not naive, Princess."

"Let them go! We have a deal!"

"The deal isn't done until we're wed."

"Where are you taking them?"

"That's none of your business," Moyen says. He turns around and walks out the gate. Annie realizes this was all planned: Moyen knew Pika was alive, he knew where Red was, and he knew he needed someone in the camp to bring peace to the kingdom. The world needs different animals to maintain order and balance—there is an ecosystem of animals that depend on one another. He just waited to see if it was Pika, Red or someone else. She looks up at the sky. It's a clear blue sky. No clouds, no birds, and the sun's off behind her in the distance. There's nothing ahead of her.

Annie turns to Moyen and yells after him, "Then, I'll stay here until the wedding!"

Moyen stops, turns and snarls, "What did you say?"

"You heard me. I'm staying here until the wedding."

"That's not the deal."

"The deal is to get married. You said nothing about where I lived until then."

Moyen walks up to Annie and puts his face into hers. He heaves several deep breaths. He says, "You think you're so smart. Fine. Stay here. The wedding is in three days. Your brother and Red will stay with me."

24. A SIMPLER PLAN

Annie and I sit in our hut. Her tunnel has been sealed by Moyen's army. The two of us sit in silence. Suspecting the guards outside are listening to us, Annie motions me to walk outside. The guards outside our hut stare at us. Annie glares at them. We walk towards the fields as they follow us. Annie whispers, "I'm leaving tonight."

"How?"

"I'll dig another tunnel."

"What about Pika, Red and us? They'll kill us if they find you missing."

"No, they won't. Moyen wants me to secure peace. He doesn't want all the rebels to die. He needs us to keep the ecosystem alive. There is no balance now, and the forest will die. He knows I won't come back if any of you are dead."

"Are you sure?"

"I'm very sure. He just wants peace. He doesn't love me. I'm his ticket to peace."

"Where are you going? Are you getting Pika and Red?"

"No, I'm going to find that unicorn. It's our only chance. I still believe in it."

We walk back to our hut. When all the lights are out, we walk out and sneak into the dining hall. From there, Annie goes under a table and starts to dig. I cover up the hole as I climb inside. I stay behind Annie, so she doesn't know I'm following. Annie burrows like crazy. She stays focused and continuously shovels with her hands. When they get tired, she sits and uses her feet to dig. She switches between her hands and feet over and over again and again until she feels she's far away enough to take a breath, and then she starts again, digging and digging like a hungry dog burrowing for bones.

Annie collapses on her stomach and face—exhausted. She's not sure how long she's been digging, but she wants to be sure she's far away enough not to be caught. She also needs to make sure she gets to Cloud Mountain. With its altitude and climate, Moyen and his army can't survive in Cloud Mountain. She doesn't have much time. Annie looks at the wall of dirt in front her. She takes a deep breath and starts digging.

After a long time, Annie surfaces. She scrambles up and out of the ground. She looks around. The moon's glow reflects off the rocks in front of her. The sound of water falling indicates that she's near the entrance of Cloud Mountain. No scent of Moyen and his army is in the air. Annie dashes towards the rocks and scrambles to the top. She sees Mercy Falls nearby. She climbs down and bounds in that direction.

The old familiar narrow and treacherous trail winds itself around Mother-Child Rock and Black Crane Falls. Annie nears the temple and slows down, on the lookout for any animals in Moyen's army. She slowly opens the gate. It creaks open. She steps in. She looks up and around, but doesn't see anyone. It's silent. It's scary silent. The wind blows leaves around the courtyard. She walks through the temple and its rooms. The furniture is dusty. The floor is covered with filth and dirt. Insects crawl around.

Annie peers into her old room. She remembers how she and Pika would stay up late, reminiscing about their human lives and talking about the future. She now realizes how early in this new life Pika changed. She usually talked about finding the unicorn, and he talked about his training and helping Leuca fight Moyen. Back then, she was self-absorbed and didn't really listen to him. Now, she can see more clearly.

"Annie!" I exclaim as she's reflecting on her life.

She jumps so high her head bounces off the ceiling like a ball off a floor. She turns around and sees me. We hug. She rubs her sore head.

"Naso, why'd you follow me?"

"If they find you missing, they'll take me away. They'd put me somewhere soooooo boring that I'd kill myself out of boredom. I'd probably share a jail cell with a mockingbird who'd just copy everything I said. Imagine that conversation!"

Annie smiles and hugs me again. "It's good to see you."

"We have to hurry. In the morning, they'll realize we're gone, and they'll come searching. We need more distance between us and them."

"You're right."

"Umm, Annie."

"Yes, Naso."

"Do you also know why I came?"

"No."

"You have no idea where you're going."

Annie looks confused and realizes I'm right. She only knew the unicorn was on the other side of the mountain, but she had no idea where. We laugh. Annie says, "Come on, let's go."

We run out of the temple and make our way up and around the mountain.

25. DRAGON RIDGE

As the trail winds around the back of the mountain, Annie and I stop. The mountain ridge with its ancient pines and azaleas winds its way around back towards Snow Forest like a dragon's tail. We look out at Snow Forest glimmering in the moonlight. Annie realizes Snow Forest's name comes from the shining tops of the dove trees in the moonlight. She laughs to herself. The moon is nearing the peak of its ascent, and we have a limited time before the army wakes up. We continue around the back of the mountain.

The rock and gravel laden trail hugs the cliffs and moves up and down like a bony spine. We stop and see the trail ends up ahead at a gigantic cliff. We slowly approach the edge and look down. The cliff drops all the way down to the river in the valley below.

"It must be thousands of feet down," I whisper and gulp.

"It could be worse."

"How do you mean?"

"We could be sharing a jail with a mockingbird," Annie says and smiles. "Come on, let's go."

Annie walks back to the mountain and slowly climbs down the rocks. I watch her and soon follow. We hop from rock to rock, and cling to shrubs and trees to break our falls. Half-way down, rocks come hurling at us. Annie yells, "Naso, hide in that split!"

We scramble into a slight opening in the mountain. Rocks continue to tumble. I ask, "Do you think it's Moyen?"

"No, they couldn't get here that fast. At least, I don't think they can," replies Annie.

The flying rocks stop. Annie peeks out and doesn't see anyone. As she lowers herself back down, a loud shriek blasts our ears. It surprises and scares Annie. She falls back into the hole. I look up and see a familiar golden orange haired monkey with giant black eyes and a blue face. It's Rhino. His snarls and many small sharp teeth frighten me. He paces around the rim of the hole. I hide behind Annie who is shaking off her headache. Annie looks up and sees the monkey. She says, "Who are you? We come in peace. We mean no harm."

I whisper, "It's Rhino. The one who fought Pika long ago."

Annie remembers. The monkey shrieks again. We cover our ears. Rhino looks up into the sky and howls. Annie aims and throws a rock that hits him in the head. He falls backwards. She clambers up the hole and finds him shaking his head. She grabs Rhino by the face. She snaps, "Why are you throwing rocks at us?"

Rhino glares at her. He bites her hands. She yells in pain. She drops him. Rhino jumps backwards. He hisses and scampers off. Annie helps me out of the hole. We dust ourselves off. Annie says, "I have no idea what just happened."

"We must have offended him."

"I don't know. Maybe something worse."

We find another trail that will take us down the mountain. Looking out, I see this spiny ridge led us to this peak that looks like the head of a dragon. Out beyond, I see the dark green forest and the burnt yellow desert. Behind the tree line, the sun is starting to rise. We move faster. Near the bottom of the mountain, the rocks turn into boulders, and then the boulders vanish into the dirt as trees start to burst out of the earth. Large cedars and firs are like curtains in front of us. We're tired and thirsty. We're hungry. We're sleepy. But we know we can't rest.

We find a trail in the forest and hike along it. After a short distance, the trees yield to a clearing with a sparkling teal lake. As we come out of the forest, we see a large group of monkeys and cranes waiting for us. Annie says, "Wait here. Rhino must've signaled them with his shrieks. I'll see what they want."

Annie slowly walks towards them. She says, "We come in peace. We don't mean any harm. It's us, Naso and Annie. We were with you in the temple before the war."

A snow white crane with a red head and black neck says, "Good to see you again."

"Onensis, is that you?"

"Yes. We've heard about you, Annie. Thank you for all you've done."

"I don't know what you're talking about."

Onensis approaches Annie and says, "Yes, you do. You've given us...hope, the most important emotion we need in desperate times."

"Why did Rhino throw rocks at us?"

Onensis turns around and looks at the crowd of monkeys. He says, "I don't know. He's not here, so I can't ask him." He pauses and asks, "You're seeking the unicorn?"

"Yes, how did you know?"

Before he answers, I leap up in front of her. I had squirmed my way through the crowd. He smiles and laughs. "Naso! Long time no see!"

Onensis turns back to Annie and asks, "Annie, why are you seeking the unicorn?"

"To save us."

"How?"

"I'll ask it to..."

"It doesn't work that way."

"What do you mean? What do I ask? Isn't it supposed to give us a wish?"

Onensis replies, "How would you feel if you spent your whole life being chased and the only reason was for giving wishes? Now, if this was true—this power that is—then why would you give people this quite generous gift? And for what in return?"

Annie lowers her head, thinking the unicorn has no powers.

The crane continues, "If an animal existed that could grant wishes, wouldn't it grant itself a wish or two? Wouldn't it be emperor or empress of the world? Wouldn't it make all animals serve it?"

Annie didn't know how to respond. I whisper to Annie, "Do you think it's true? The unicorn has no powers?"

Annie nods. She approaches Onensis and asks, "How do you know all these things?"

"Does it matter?"

I then realize the cranes and monkeys are all living in the forest—they usually live in the mountains and in the temple. I ask, "Why are you down here? This isn't your home."

Onensis answers, "Good observation, young one."

A loud commotion erupts from the crowd. The monkeys start shrieking, and the cranes start flapping their wings. Rhino bounds down the mountain with short, sharp howls. Onensis yells, "We must leave! Moyen's army is coming up the mountain. They'll be here anytime."

The cranes break into several lines, and line-by-line they fly into the air, led by the old short crane. The monkeys scatter into the trees, and leap from tree top to tree top. Soon, Annie and I are alone. We run back to the trail and dash through the forest.

26. RHINO

I look back and see Moyen's army at the top of the mountain starting their descent. We didn't think they could summit the mountain and make it out this far. General Mantchu with his long

113

white mustache leads an envoy of dholes and cougars. Moyen is nowhere to be seen. My tiny little feet run as fast as they can—after all the months in prison, they're thin and worn, bruised and calloused. Because I've been awake for a long time, I'm hungry and tired. I push myself, but I can't keep it up for long.

Every now and then, Annie checks on me, but her mind is occupied with the unicorn. What if Onensis is right about the unicorn? What if this is all hopeless? Should she just go back and stop this ridiculous plan? Should she just sacrifice herself for the peace of the kingdom? But she'll be miserable. She can't live that way.

All these thoughts consume Annie. She isn't paying attention and trips over a tree root. She's flung several feet and tumbles over herself. I run to her side and ask, "Are you alright? Are you hurt?"

Annie sits up, crying.

"You're hurt! Where? How bad is it?"

"No," Annie says. "I'm not hurt. I don't know what the point of this is anymore. Let's go back."

"We can't! You can't ruin your life!"

"I'll just ruin everyone else's. It's fine."

"No! Onensis is wrong."

"How do you know?"

"I don't know. But it's our only hope."

"That's the whole point. It's our only hope because we believed in it. There's one other option." Annie looks at me, and I know what she's thinking.

"No! You're not giving yourself up! Come on, get up! Let's go!"

Annie continues to sit and cry. After she wipes her tears on her arms, she looks at her hands. She's still some mix of real rabbit and stuffed animal. She longs to be human again. She wants to be home with her brother, her father and her mother. She wants a chance to tell her mother 'sorry'. She wants to tell her father 'sorry' for causing his death. She wants her family back. All these emotions and thoughts pour through her mind. She falls back and stares at the sky with tears filling up her eyes like buckets of rain.

While eying General Mantchu in the distance, I tug Annie and scream, "They're coming down! They'll be here any minute now! Let's go!"

"Ow!" yells Annie as a rock smashes into her stomach, and she falls back. I look around. Rhino swings from the trees and lands in front of us.

He mutters, "Get up. Get out of here. You led them to us!"

Annie asks, "Why are you throwing rocks at us?"

He puts his face in hers and says, "They say you're the one. I don't see it. Stupid. You led them to us!"

"What are you talking about?"

"You can't handle little rocks," he says. He turns around, walks off and mutters to himself. "I knew it. Stupid animals. Always believing in stuff. I'm the smart one. Not gullible like them. Always throwing themselves at the first thing. What do they do to me? Kick me out. Stupid animals. Gullible. No brains. That's right. Me, I'm smart."

Annie gets up and chases after him. I follow along. Quick and agile, he maneuvers around trees and boulders, not stopping for anything. We constantly look up for him and struggle to keep up on the ground. Annie yells out, "Stop! You're losing us!"

Rhino swings to a branch and stops. Perching on it, he has an angry puzzled look on his face. He purses his lips and sighs. "Hurry up!" he yells. "They're catching up."

He swings from branch to branch down to them. He lands in front of them, and he says, "Never get away. Too slow. Army too fast. New plan!"

Annie asks, "Why aren't you with all the other monkeys?"

"Chit-chat's stupid. They'll be here anytime. Go, go, go."

"You said we can't get away fast enough. What should we do?"

Rhino looks around and says, "Go underground. I'll follow. Never get ahead on foot. Dig many tunnels—one real, many fake. Hurry!"

Annie and I start digging out tunnels that lead nowhere. We dig down into the earth, come back out, dig another hole, and repeat this over and over. After several holes are made, Rhino covers them with leaves and dirt to trick the army. Then Annie starts digging our main tunnel. Rhino covers it up as he climbs in.

Annie and I dig together. Rhino follows behind, guarding us. Annie asks, "Rhino, do you know where we're going?"

"Dragon Desert."

"How'd you know?"

"Brain."

"Is that where the unicorn lives?"

"Don't know. You tell me," he replies.

"We're going to find the unicorn to save the animals."

"How?"

"I'll ask it to change Pika and myself back to humans. Pika will free Red and escape. I'll get other humans to come and rescue everyone."

Rhino says, "Humans won't save us. Don't care. Kill animals. Don't save us."

"They will. I'll tell them what's happened."

He laughs, "You and Pika—go back old lives. Forget us."

"No, I promise you."

Rhino pauses and then says, "What if no miracles?"

Annie stops digging and puts her hand on my shoulder. I stop. Annie looks at Rhino. She asks, "Why are you here? Why did you throw rocks at us?"

Rhino says, "Dig, dig, dig. Talk if you dig."

Annie and I start digging again. Rhino continues, "Betrayed by brothers and sisters. Onensis, cranes, monkeys were mad. Leuca grew closer to Pika. Day by day. Cloud Mountain is temple of immortals. Only the purest of souls live there. Cranes lived and ruled from beginning. Monkeys protect and serve. Moyen grew powerful. Destroy temple."

"Why?" asks Annie.

"All looked to the cranes for guidance. Not Moyen. Filled him with hatred."

I say, "So he wanted the temple destroyed."

"Yes," replies Rhino. "Cranes needed help. Searched out legend spirit, Leuca. He doesn't fight. But he knows how. Leuca unmatched. Even Moyen respected Leuca. Took long time, but Leuca joined. He never wanted battle. Peaceful he is."

We quiet down. We hear the trample of feet above on the surface. We know the army is nearby now. They've descended the mountain. They probably haven't discovered the tunnels yet. We have little time to lose. Annie and I dig faster, and we all stop talking.

Rhino follows us close behind. His eyes don't see well in the dark. Anxious and nervous, he doesn't like being underground and in closed quarters—he's claustrophobic and likes open air. When the footsteps disappear, Rhino continues with his story. "Born in the temple. All I ever know. Raised to be warrior and to protect the temple. At all costs. Cranes trained me first. Then Leuca. I was his favorite…then Pika."

"And that's why you fought him," says Annie.

"No. Set up."

"What?" I ask surprised.

"I'm trained warrior. See myself clearly. Always someone better than you. Face that, we must. Pika is better, I'm ok. But test his heart and his mind we must."

"It was a test?" asks Annie.

"Yes. Night before. Leuca, Red and I made plans. See how Pika respond. Test his skills. Pika did great. We all proud."

"I didn't see you at the battle. What happened?" asks Annie.

"No others knew. Me disgraced. Cranes and monkeys angry with Leuca and Pika. Back at room. Monkeys beat me," Rhino says with his voice trailing off. He pauses for a while. Then he continues, "Monkeys tied me. Brought me out. Onensis embarrassed for me. I was humiliated. Left that night. Stayed in mountains ever since. Watched the battle. Heard pain. But...watched you lead and give hope."

Annie looks at his face full of sorrow. I hold his hand, and he pulls it back. He says, "No sympathy. Made my choice."

Annie asks, "I don't understand why you threw rocks at us."

"Watched everything far away. I know Pika; don't know you," Rhino says. He shrugs his shoulder and says, "Bad test."

Annie and I laugh. She says, "Well then, I guess we make a good team. None of us seem to do anything right."

27. TRAP

"Go up now," says Rhino.

Annie digs up to the surface. We hop out of the hole. We are surrounded by Moyen's army. General Mantchu walks up to us and says, "Brother Rhino! Brother Rhino!"

Annie and I are shocked and dumbfounded. We don't know what to say. We look at Rhino who merely shrugs and walks next to General Mantchu. He whispers something into the General's ear. He looks at us and says, "All is true. Never finished story. But you figure out."

General Mantchu says, "Annie, wedding now."

"What about Naso?"

"Back to camp."

"You won't hurt her?"

General Mantchu slowly and clearly says, "Of course not."

"I don't believe you."

"Me kill her now. You too. But Moyen no. Peace. Legacy. Come now. You fight, deal off."

"What if I don't go?"

"Shut up. Just marry. Be done. Wasted time. Guards! Take her. Forget mouse. Me not care."

Annie surveys the terrain—scattered firs and cedars with large boulders in between. She quickly estimates around twenty dholes and cougars. As two large dholes approach her, she leaps up and spin kicks them. Their heads snap back, and they collapse. She yells at me, "Naso, hide!"

She takes a sword from each of the fallen dholes. She jumps with the swords like a whirling hurricane. She hits a couple more soldiers. General Mantchu steps back and pulls his steel ninja stars out of his horse's back pack. He launches them at Annie who deflects them with her sword. One of the stars sticks into a cougar's forehead. General Mantchu yells for the soldiers to attack. A few cougars surround her. She quickly burrows into the ground and digs holes underneath their feet. They fall into a deep hole where she buries them up to their necks. She turns around and sees Rhino staring at her. He grabs the swords from her. She trips and tries to backpedal towards a boulder. He whispers, "Believe you now. Passed test. Follow me."

Rhino spins around and lunges at the remaining soldiers. With the swords, he cuts down two dholes, and his tail swipes another dhole's staff. Annie follows Rhino. He leaps onto his tail. With his feet, he swipes two more swords and tosses them to Annie. While he fights the dholes and cougars, General Mantchu sneaks behind Annie and grabs her. He takes a sword and cuts her shoulder as she breaks free. She looks down at the blood flowing from her shoulder to her forearm. She grasps it to stop the bleeding. General Mantchu opens up his tail feathers, enveloping her in darkness. The pattern of his feather camouflages him, and she gets a headache. She feels dizzy. There must be some magic spell. She's punched in the face. She's punched in the stomach. She falls down. Looking around, she can't see him, just an ocean of feathers. As she stumbles around, lunging and punching the air, he laughs. Suddenly, she's snatched and slung in the air by her long ears. She feels a cold steel blade against her neck. General Mantchu hisses, "This too easy."

He hits her hard on the head with the blunt edge of the sword. She's knocked out. He picks her up and throws her on his horse. As he prepares to mount the horse, his feet are pulled out. He falls onto his stomach. He scrambles back to his feet. He looks around and yells, "Rhino! Traitor! Fight with courage. Coward! Kill you now!"

Rhino lands in front of him. General Mantchu snickers. Rhino holds his two swords and charges. General Mantchu easily blocks him and knocks him to the ground. He throws his feather tail back up. Rhino tries to find Mantchu in the wall of feathers. As the camouflage starts to make him dizzy, he gets hit from all sides. Falling to the ground, he knows Mantchu must be in the middle somewhere, but the feathers blur distance and perception. He looks at the ground and grabs rocks with his hands and feet. He leans back on his tail, spins and throws rocks in all directions.

"Ow!" screams Mantchu. The feather wall comes down as the feathers fold back into the tail. General Mantchu is hunched over the ground. Rhino leaps and kicks him over. Grabbing General Mantchu's mustache, Rhino hurls him against a boulder. After Rhino kicks him in the stomach and the cheek, he grabs a sword and cuts off Mantchu's right wing. General Mantchu screams and writhes in pain. Blood pours out. He covers his shoulder where his wing used to be. He grabs dirt and stuffs it in the hole to stop the bleeding. He tries to stand but falls over. The pain is too much as he thrashes across the ground like a snake with its head cut off.

Rhino says, "Take message back: destroy you all."

Taking the weapons, Rhino tosses them into a hole. He leaps onto General Mantchu's horse where Annie still lays. He guides the horse over to a large boulder where I'm hiding. He says, "Come Naso. Got ride now. No worry, trust me now. Come on."

I look around and can't decide. I see Annie and decide to stay with her. Snatching us up, Rhino sets us in front of him. Rhino whips the reins, and the horse races through the forest into the desert.

28. DRAGON DESERT

The trees and rocks trail off. Vast sand dunes shaped like dragons appear before our eyes. Rhino stops the horse. After we dismount, Annie yells, "What was that about? Who are you? What side are you on?"

She punches him in the chest, and Rhino steps back. He says, "Stop. Deserve that one. Same side. Trust you now."

I throw sand at him and scream, "Why'd you betray us? You took us right to them."

"Had to."

I yell, "Liar! You just switch sides when it's convenient for you. You only care about saving your own skin."

"No. Easy way is kill you two. This is hard way."

Annie lunges and knocks Rhino over. She chokes him, and he knocks her off. He says, "See here. We never outrun them. I had plan. You never believe. It worked."

I punch Rhino's back—it's hard like a sack of rocks. I take my long tail and wrap it around his throat. He pulls my tail off and says, "Stop. Here now. Find unicorn."

Annie and I sit in the sand. We're confused. Adrenalin is rushing through our blood. We're all worked up. Rhino says, "Mantchu going back to Moyen. Moyen will do terrible things. No time to lose."

"Why didn't you kill General Mantchu?" asks Annie.

"Deliver message to Moyen."

"Wait, why did he say 'thank you Rhino'? It was a plan. This is all part of the plan."

"No. They found me in mountains. Deal made. Never would let them take you. Need you." Rhino pauses and then adds, "For hope."

"Something's not right."

"Believe me," says Rhino.

"If you're on our side, then stay here. Naso and I will go find the unicorn. If you come after us, then I'll kill you."

"You won't survive alone. I come."

"Aha!" exclaims Annie.

"What?"

"I can't trust you. You're up to something. I don't know what, but I know you're up to something."

"Not," pleads Rhino. He gets frustrated and walks back to the horse. "Take horse. I wait."

I ask, "Is this part of the trick?"

Annie and I are confused. We don't know what to believe anymore. Annie says, "We're going on foot. Stay here with the horse. If you believe in me, then stay here."

"Fine," snarls Rhino.

Annie and I walk up the sand dune that's as tall as a pine tree. We watch Rhino disappear in the distance. I whisper, "I don't trust him."

"Neither do I."

"What should we do?"

"I don't know. I need some time to think. How do we find the unicorn?"

"They say you can find her by a dead tree fallen over a stream."

We stand at the top of the sand dune and look out. All we see is sand—sand dunes carved by the wind like dragons flying into the world away from the sun. No trees, no shrubs, and definitely no water. We look at one another. We each look defeated. The sun is hot. Our skin boils underneath our fur. We have to find shade soon. Annie wishes she took the horse. She thinks about the fallen tree over a stream. She keeps looking but doesn't see anything. She asks me, "What if it's a riddle?"

"What are you talking about?"

"What if it's not really a tree and a stream, but what if it means something else?"

"I wouldn't know what. It sounds pretty literal. Find a dead tree fallen over a stream."

Annie mutters to herself, "Dead tree. Dead tree. Stream. Dead tree. Stream. Water. Dragon desert. Sand, tree, mud, dirt. Ugh, I don't know. Desert."

Annie walks around the mound of sand, mumbling to herself and yanking her ears all around. She kicks the sand. She gazes up at the sky. I should help her think, but I have no clue. I'm just amused watching her.

"That's it!" Annie grabs me and says, "This is the desert. There's no water out here. There's no stream. We can see that. Dead tree. If there was a stream, the tree would be alive, right? Trees need water. But this is a desert. The only time there's rivers and streams is when it rains. We have to find a dead tree where a stream used to be. When it rains, that's where the unicorn will appear."

"You're right! That makes sense!" I reply confidently and wholeheartedly, but I really have no idea.

We look around for fallen dead trees. We don't see anything. Annie leads us to another sand dune. We continue hiking up and down sand dunes to scout the area. We finally get to a sand dune where I spot something. I yell, "I see it! Over there!"

I point to a dead cedar lying in a valley between two sand dunes. We run down the dune and around the winding hills until we get to the tree. The trunk is white and dry. The wood is brittle. Only half of the tree remains, and the trunk has been hollowed out. Several long dry branches stretch out. It doesn't seem like it's rained in a long time. The sand under the tree is dry, and only dead shrubs lay around. We look up at the sky. Not a cloud above. A slight wind blows. Occasionally, sand gets in our eyes, and we have to rub it out.

"What do we do, Annie?"

"I don't know."

We sit on the log, unsure of anything. Only the sound of a soft wind sweeping across the sands can be heard. The sun is slowly sinking, and the shadow of the sand dune provides a relief from the sun's heat. We're thirsty, and we're getting hungry. There are no plants or anything else to eat.

"We can't sit here until it rains," I comment.

"I know."

"What are we going to do?"

"I don't know."

"At night, the desert will be freezing."

123

"I forgot about that," Annie says.

"We have to move on. This probably isn't it."

"No, I'm sure this is it. What did they tell you?"

"The unicorn can be found by a dead tree fallen over a stream."

"Did they say what type of stream?"

"What do you mean? A stream. A stream is a stream."

"Well, a stream of water?"

"Of course."

"It could've been a stream of light, or a stream of people, or a stream of animals."

"A tree wouldn't fall over a stream of animals."

Annie thinks and tries to remember all the stories about unicorns. She thinks about the paintings she saw as a child. She asks me, "Do unicorns only appear at night?"

"Hmmm, I don't know."

"I don't remember any paintings of unicorns at daytime. Unicorns are always drawn with the moon and stars surrounding them."

"We don't have paintings. No one really asks about the unicorns. They usually ask about the miracles."

"When my mother died, they say a unicorn crossed the moonlit sky on a cloud of flames."

"She must've been an amazing person if a unicorn appeared."

"She was," Annie quietly says and pauses for a few minutes. She wipes her eyes before continuing, "She really was. I was just too dumb to realize it. I spent my life chasing the wrong things. She was always there, and I just didn't see it."

I didn't know what to say, so I gave Annie a long hug. She smiles and asks, "Where does the moon come up?"

I look around and point to the opening between the two sand dunes. Annie jumps up and hugs me. "This is it! A dead tree fallen over a stream...of moonlight. Look! The moon will come up from there. The moonlight would flow through this canyon and across this fallen tree. It's not a stream of water, but a stream of moonlight."

"Are you sure?"

"I'm positive!" Annie grabs me and dances around. She collapses in excitement. "Let's get some rest. We have a busy night."

29. QILIN

The temperature changes dramatically as the sun sets. The hot boil of the sun changes to a bitter chilling wind. Annie and I shiver in the biting cold wind. I ask, "Are you still planning to ask the unicorn to turn you and Pika back to humans?"

"Yes, only when we're human can we save all this."

"Is that the only way?"

"I can't think of another way," Annie says.

"Just ask for peace and freedom."

"That's not a solution. We have to ask for specifics. The unicorn won't know what to do with 'peace and freedom'. You can argue that there's peace under Moyen."

"I suppose you're right. I'm going to miss you."

"Don't worry, I'm not going anywhere. I won't forget you. When this is all over, you'll come and stay with me and Pika," Annie replies comforting me.

"That's nice, but we know it's not true."

"Why do you say that?"

"We both know it's not going to happen that way. We'll each go back to our own lives. Humans and animals don't co-exist."

"Yes, they do. We live with horses, dogs and sheep."

I shrug and say, "They serve you. They're not equal. You even eat some."

"Look at us. We're friends."

"You're not a human now. It'll be different when you're back to a human."

Annie hugs me and promises not to change. She says, "Naso, don't worry. I've learned a lot and have changed. I wouldn't be alive without you."

The sun vanishes behind the sand dune, and the sky darkens, revealing a blanket of twinkling stars like the eyes of grasshoppers peeking out from underneath a blanket of leaves. The moon's glow starts to stream through the canyons across the sand dunes. The sand sparkles like rubies and gleams in the light. The light looks like a river ebbing its way down the canyon—fingers reaching out and grasping for more and more sand. Soon, we are draped in the blue-white glow of the moon. The area around us comes to life. We think that we see fireflies, but it's only the sparkles of the light.

Then, I see her. I can't believe my eyes. I rub them. Annie just stares. Following the path of the moonlight, a unicorn appears in the distant canyon and strolls down towards us. It seems to drink from the moonlight. As it approaches us, Annie's heart beats faster and faster. She's finally going to turn back to a human. She'll find her brother. Then everything will be back to normal.

The Chinese unicorn is larger than either one of us imagined. The unicorn stands about fifteen tigers tall—her head looks out over the dunes. She walks slowly and gracefully. Every step is taken full of thought and purpose. The unicorn's red burning fire around its mane and tail glows and seems to radiate a heavenly brilliance. Her antlers shine and look like they reach into the heavens, holding them up. With each step, her hoof leaves a soft print in the sand which the wind blows away into the sky. The unicorn approaches Annie and me. She leans her neck down and closes her eyes as if she's bowing before us. We are mesmerized by her presence and are speechless. Her dragon face doesn't scare us, rather the face seems child-like. The golden scales across her body glimmer like a lake under the moon. We've never seen an animal so beautiful, so peaceful and so full of purpose.

At this moment, Annie forgets all her problems. Watching the unicorn, Annie doesn't know why or how, but she wants to be like her. She wants to carry the same sense of purpose and have others see that in her. She looks the unicorn all over, and admires its beauty and perfection.

The unicorn turns towards Annie and says, "I sense you have come a long way and have something to ask."

"How do you know?"

"This world is old. When you live as long as I have, you learn much through experience. There isn't really much new under this moon. What is your name?"

"I'm Annie, and this is Naso," says Annie, kowtowing. I hop over and bow my head. Annie continues, "We came from Snow Forest to find you. We need your help."

"My name is Qilin. What is it that you need? I'm of little use these days. This is my world, and yours is so far away. I suspect Moyen is up to no good."

"Yes, how did you know?"

"Animals are hard to change; spirits are even harder. He set himself in his ways, and only he can change his path."

I interrupt and cry, "He killed Leuca!"

Qilin steps back and is surprised. She looks up at the sky and the stars. She looks back at them and says, "I sensed a change. I didn't know what it was. I was brought out of my sleep one night. How did it happen? Why?"

I quickly and incoherently blurted out, "Onensis. It was his idea. Leuca didn't want to be involved. But we lost before. And then we needed help. Onensis didn't know what to do. He's a coward! The animals convinced Leuca to join the battle. Up in the temple at Cloud Mountain, we trained and prepared. Leuca led us into battle. It was horrible! So horrible! Everyone died! Moyen killed him. It was sooooooo horrible!"

Qilin says, "That is why I came out of my sleep. But now, another change is coming. I have been asleep for several months. Something else has awaken me tonight."

I nudge Annie and whisper, "Ask her. It's time."

She looks confused and asks, "Did you know my mother?"

Qilin gently smiles. She takes a long breath and replies, "I once awoke when a strong and courageous woman passed away out of sadness. She provided her people hope. It's very special, you know. Hope. It keeps most of us around. But she lost her own hope, and then we lost her."

Annie falls to her knees and cries. She wipes away her tears and says, "It's my fault. She wanted to see me, but I never went. I'm horrible. I'll never forgive myself."

Qilin nudges Annie's chin up and says, "Those who can't forgive don't believe in hope."

"She died because of me!"

"No, she died because she lost faith in herself and in others. We all choose our paths and live out our journeys. Every moment is a choice. We can't choose for others, but you can choose for yourself. What is your path?"

"I don't know."

"One more question. Are we talking about the same person? Or did you assume you knew who I was talking about? You never asked me."

Annie realizes she assumed the woman was her mother, and all the guilt she carried these years just came out. Annie looks at Qilin and then myself. She wipes her tears away and walks up the sand dune. Looking out across the desert, she takes several deep breaths. She closes her eyes and remembers her mother's face. Annie does have a choice, and she takes one more deep breath. She walks back down to us.

Annie nervously asks, "Qilin, I don't mean any disrespect, but we hear you grant wishes. We have one to ask."

Qilin laughs and says, "This is what they say of me? Ha ha. You think I can grant wishes. Would you like riches and money?"

"No, I want to be human again."

Qilin lowers her neck and stares into Annie's eyes. Qilin asks, "Do you feel anything?"

"No."

"Good."

"What?"

"Good," says Qilin. She stands back up and continues, "I don't grant wishes. I don't make wishes come true. I don't know magic nor any spells."

"But…"

"There are many myths in these forests, valleys and mountains. Animals will say what they want others to believe. Or animals will believe what they want to believe. I'm sorry, but I can't break your spell. Only you can."

"All the animals who found you before…."

"I don't know what they said. Sometimes it's better to keep a stone rolling than to stop it, especially a large one," Qilin says before pausing. She turns and faces the moon. She says, "Look at the moon, it gives us a purpose each day. We look forward to its rising. And with it, we also look forward to the sun. Days and nights pass like this. For thousands of years, it has been so. Just as you are here today, you will be gone one day. In the short time we are here, we have to find our purpose. Annie, you are just a child. You have many more moons and suns to see. All I know is that myths are told to give purpose. With me, did you find a purpose?"

Annie shakes her head. Qilin kneels and puts her hoof around Annie's shoulder. She says, "I sense you felt something when you first saw me. Remember that feeling. You have a purpose. You may not know what it is now, but you will find it."

Annie is quiet. I ask, "But Qilin, we don't have time. The animals are imprisoned. Moyen took Annie's brother, and he took Red. They'll all die soon."

Qilin is surprised and says, "They took Red? The situation indeed is terrible. Unfortunately, there isn't anything I can do. As I said, I don't have magical powers. All the magic is in you. The world must move forward untethered. I can't move it one direction or another. I must let things play out as they are meant to. Spirits are great and terrible beings. Moyen cannot be easily defeated. It will take someone of great courage and mind to defeat him."

I ask, "Isn't there anything you can do? Why are you here?"

"Why are you here? It's a good question for all of us. I sleep in the heavens and travel the stars at night. I'm awakened when the spirits summon me either with the passing or the coming of great joy. I never know what the situation or the circumstances are. I'm fortunate sometimes to find someone here. Often, I'm alone, and I can only guess what the situation is. So, I fly the skies at night, hoping to see what just may be the reason why I wake from my sleep."

Annie asks, "Why have you come this time?"

"I never know," Qilin answers. She touches Annie's nose with her hoof. She says, "I sense a great joy will be coming. I have much enjoyed this conversation. I won't need to fly tonight."

Qilin turns around and walks back through the canyon. She turns around and says, "Your mother found a purpose and then lost it. Please don't lose yours."

Fire surrounds Qilin, and it burns brighter and brighter. The stream of moonlight follows her out of the canyon. Soon the fire and Qilin vanish, and the canyon is dark with only the stars shining up above.

30. HOME

"We're going to die! It's hopeless!" I shout. I lay in the sand crying and throwing a tantrum. I pound the sand with my hands.

Annie walks over and says, "Calm down, calm down."

"I can't! We came all the way out here, and she won't help us! We're going to die, and then all the animals will die! Moyen's going to destroy us all."

"It didn't turn out the way we wanted, but we still have to hope."

"Hope? I don't get you. You're still not human. How are you going to turn back to human? And what did she mean by all that purpose and joy talk? That's completely useless."

Annie pulls me up by the shoulders. She stares into my face and says, "Calm down, we'll find a way."

"I'm sorry Annie, but it feels hopeless. We're stuck in the desert with no food and no water. It's freezing. We're going to turn into ice. Our friends are dying in a camp, or they're dead! Moyen has your brother and Red. You have to marry him to save us. I'm sorry Annie, but there isn't any way out."

"Let's head back before the cold kills us," Annie says. She stops to hug me and adds, "Naso, aren't you supposed to be the happy and fun one? I'm the dramatic one. How are we going to make it if I have to be fun one?"

We both laugh. I reply, "Alright, let's go."

We track our way back through the desert to the edge of the forest. Rhino is sleeping under a boulder. Annie walks up to Rhino and pokes him. She says, "Rhino, wake up. Wake up."

He mutters and growls. Blinking and rubbing his eyes, he says, "Back?"

I answer, "We've been gone a long time."

"Not that long. Find her?" he asks. He looks at Annie and says, "Guess not. Still rabbit."

I respond, "We found her. But she didn't help us."

Rhino sits up, intrigued. He says, "Really? Didn't believe she lived."

"Yes, we found her. She said she doesn't grant wishes. She doesn't help. She's some sort of symbol of stuff. Ugh, so frustrating," I complain.

Rhino looks at Annie and says, "Quiet. What happened?"

"I don't know. Naso's right, we found her."

"Not human?"

"No. How far back to Snow Forest?"

"Day. Faster with Moyen chasing. Dig tunnel to go faster. But earth is rocky and hard."

Annie is quiet and thinks. I'm eager to get going. Rhino grabs some leaves off a shrub and hands them out to eat. "Eat. I find water. Then we go."

Rhino runs into the forest. Annie and I munch on the leaves. When Rhino returns, we drink water and begin hiking through the forest. He asks, "Back to temple?"

Annie looks at Rhino and asks, "Why are you with us? Why didn't you leave?"

"Not with you. Just against Moyen."

"That's good enough. We're going straight until we run into Moyen's army."

"What?"

"You heard me. We're going until we run into them."

I ask, "How are we going to fight them? There's only three of us. They'll probably have hundreds."

Annie replies, "We're not fighting them. We'll let them take us."

Rhino stops and says, "Wait. Let them? Makes no sense. Free now."

Annie says, "You can leave if you want. That's the plan."

"Don't get it."

I say, "I don't either. Why would we get captured again? How would we free Pika and Red?"

"When Moyen marries me, everyone will be freed."

"But we'll all be under his tyranny," I say. "That's not a plan."

Rhino yells, "Stupid! No capture!"

"You two don't have to go with me. That's my plan."

I say, "Fine, I'll go with you. You're my family."

Annie hugs me and says, "Thank you."

Rhino says, "Go until we see them. Then I go."

Annie says, "That's fine."

31. CAGED HOPE

In the heart of the forest, we hear the trampling feet of Moyen's army. Rhino wishes Annie and me luck and swings off into the trees. Annie and I move forward until we arrive near the lake where we first met the cranes and monkeys. We eat some plants and drink water from a nearby stream. The first person we see is Moyen who is leading the army himself. Behind him, a wingless General Mantchu rides a horse. Moyen spots us and walks over.

Moyen smirks, "So much trouble for such a little girl."

General Mantchu yells, "Kill them!"

Moyen laughs and says, "No, I love that instinct for my empress. Now, let there be no more trouble. Otherwise, I certainly will kill Pika and Red. This time, you are staying at my palace where I can watch you."

Annie asks, "What about Naso?"

"She'll go back to camp. I have no use for her."

"I want her with me. She's my best friend."

"Oh, how sweet, but no. You two have caused enough trouble. The wedding will be tomorrow. Your friend will be freed after that."

The guards tie up Annie and me, and throw Annie on the back of General Mantchu's horse and me onto another one. Moyen turns the army around and heads back up Cloud Mountain. The steep cliffs make a long treacherous ride up the mountain. Moyen easily climbs the rocks with his giant strong paws. He leaps from boulder to boulder and scales the cliff with ease. He waits at the top. His army, on the other hand, struggles. They aren't used to the terrain and altitude. They struggle to march up the mountain, losing their footing on the rocks and stopping frequently to catch their breath. General Mantchu's horse has difficulty carrying the weight of Annie and him— it keeps losing balance on the loose rocks. General Mantchu orders a soldier to dismount and put Annie next to me.

After we're moved together, Annie whispers, "Naso, this is the plan. I need you to follow it. It's our only chance."

"I knew you had a plan. You wouldn't give up so easily. What is it?"

"When you get to camp, tell the other animals that I'm alright, and we'll fight for our freedom tomorrow morning at my wedding. We don't have much time. When you get in, you and a few others have to start digging a tunnel to Cloud Mountain. With me captured, Moyen won't be expecting an escape. You have to finish the tunnel by dusk. After bedtime, everyone has to sneak out to the temple. Keep a dozen diggers around. Before midnight, you and the diggers have to burrow out holes all around the camp. Place anything sharp in them. Pour honey, sap and anything sticky in them. Cover them up with branches and leaves. Then get out to the temple."

"It will be a death trap."

"Yes, but it won't last for long. Moyen will figure it out soon. So, you have to get to the temple by midnight."

"Then what?"

"If all works out, help will arrive. Before the sun rises, you'll have to lead the descent from Cloud Mountain. I need you all to be at the edge of Snow Forest by sunrise. Everyone has to be armed. Wait for my signal."

"What's the signal?"

"I don't know. But it will be obvious."

"Annie?"

"What?"

"I'm scared."

"Me too. But we'll both be alright. I promise you," whispers Annie. She touches her forehead to mine. "I believe in you."

At the top, Moyen looks at us. He orders us to be split up. Annie is thrown back on General Mantchu's horse. The soldier on my horse rides off towards the camp. General Mantchu guides his horse down the rocky trail to Snow Forest. He yells back to Annie, "Lucky, lucky,

lucky. Value you have. Or die a hundred deaths."

"That'd be hard to do with just one wing."

"Shut up!"

"Wow, finally something I understand."

"Lucky to be alive. Just wait. Married off and then kill off. An offering."

Annie doesn't respond. She realized this long ago. Her silence bothers General Mantchu. He wants to provoke her. He yells, "Nothing? Crying and afraid. What a shame. Waste of a rabbit's body. Witch make you worm. To be squished to death. Save me all this trouble."

Annie remains silent. General Mantchu gets more and more upset. He punches her. Moyen sees that and lunges at General Mantchu. He yells, "Stop it! Leave her alone. Or I'll kill you too."

General Mantchu stops and focuses on riding. He mutters angry words to himself. Annie smiles. She says, "It's the only thing you're good at…being crazy. You nut job."

"Shut up!"

Moyen glares at General Mantchu who stops talking and quietly fumes at Annie. As they pass through the forest, she sees the bark of a tree. The bark is breaking off, but is thick and worn and torn. She sees the sap leaking out. The tree reaches far up into the heavens. She can't even see the top. The branches reach far out. The pine needles wave in the wind. She wonders how they stay on. It's amazing. The wind, the sun, the rain, and all these other things—the tree bends but never breaks. She remembers Qilin. She remembers when she first saw Qilin. The peacefulness and purpose with which she walked inspired her. Such a magnificent and giant beast walked like a butterfly, barely touching the ground and leaving no trace of its ever being there. Her fire glowed but didn't burn.

As the sun sets, they enter Moyen's palace. Two giant wooden gates open and reveal a magnificent field of grass and fluorescent flowers surrounded by lofty firs where houses have been built on top of them. Wooden slack bridges connect the tree houses to one another. Annie's never seen anything like it. Torches light up the palace and flicker against the dark wood, creating a nice warm mood. Animals walk around peacefully, laughing and talking. They all greet Moyen and General Mantchu. The conversations are casual and familiar. They aren't cold and calculated as she expected. Children playing and laughing surprises her. She expected a dark cold cave where animals were starved and tortured. Instead, she sees a place where animals seem happy.

"Where's Pika and Red? I want to see them," Annie says.

"Tomorrow," answers Moyen. "You'll see them all tomorrow."

"No, I want to see them now. I won't marry you until I know they are fine."

Moyen motions to General Mantchu to take her to them. General Mantchu leads her through the palace of trees to a tree surrounded by stinging needles and sharp spears. He motions to a soldier to lower a cage. Annie sees Pika and Red. She carefully squeezes past the spears to the cage. Grabbing her brother's hands, she puts them on her face. Through the cage, she touches their cheeks. Pika and Annie cry. Annie asks, "Are you alright?"

"Yes, you?"

"Yes. Red?"

"Yes," answers Red who has grown frail and looks near death. Red doesn't have any strength and leans against the cage.

Annie says to Pika, "Remember General Sun."

"Yes."

"Remember our last night when he took us through the tunnel?"

"I guess so, but I don't know…"

Annie winks and says, "Shhh."

Pika gets the message. The cage rattles. The guards pull the cage back up. Her face grows determined. She is focused. General Mantchu grabs her and pulls her back towards the main chambers. He leads her up a stairwell on a tree and shoves her into a small cozy room. The hardwood floors have a warm glow in the candlelight. The bed of soft grass and leaves is raised and is the closest thing to a human bed that she's had in all this time. She takes in the homely feel of the room and sighs. General Mantchu says, "Your room. Guards will kill. Don't try to die. All over tomorrow."

32. A SIMPLE PLAN

After eating dinner by herself, Annie returns to her tree house. She looks out over the palace—dholes and cougars, bears and tigers walk around the meadow, talking and enjoying themselves. Guards march across the bridges. She's so high up. Unsure of how she'll escape tonight, she plans out several ideas.

While she waits for night to settle in, she breaks off a strip of wood from the wall. Sitting on the floor, she takes a sharp stone and starts smoothing out the sides and surfaces. She pulls the stone towards her and pushes it away, back and forth. The repetitive motion helps soothe her mind and puts her at ease. She shapes the wood, so it bends a bit in the middle, and she chisels at the corners. Soon she holds up her shield, shaped like a half-ellipse. She turns it around with pride. She hammers in a strap made out of dove leaves.

She glances out the window, and it's still not dark enough. Looking over her shield, she thinks about an emblem. She doesn't want her father's emblem of a dragon wrapped around the sun. It doesn't feel like her calling anymore. Instead, she remembers Dragon Desert. She etches three stick figure dragons flying away from the sun into the world. She sets down her shield.

Watching the guards from her window, she realizes there's a pattern to their movement. As she blows out the torches and candles, her room is suddenly dark. She throws her shield on her back. She climbs up on a dresser and leaps at a beam across the ceiling. Grasping and pulling herself onto it, she perches and pulls aside the thick palm leaves above her. She sneaks out on the roof. She quietly walks along and bounds to the next roof. The thick winter yellow hair on her rabbit feet make a soft landing. Hopping across roofs, her dark silhouette is cast against the big yellow moon. She shinnies down a tree and hides behind its trunk. She sniffs for any guards. She races across the meadow to the dining hall. Upon finding a large dining table in the middle of the room, she starts to dig.

With a full meal and plenty of energy, she digs faster than she ever dug before. When Moyen captured her, she memorized the route from Mercy Falls—she had counted the number of steps it would take, and she created a map in her mind. After some time, she surfaces and finds herself at the waterfall. She hurries up the trail towards the temple.

When she arrives, the camp animals have all escaped through our tunnel. I see her through the crowd and run to her. We hug. She shows me her shield, and I tell her I love it. I ask if the dragons are us—she says 'yes'. I smile. She tells us all to eat and drink—we need all our energy tomorrow. In the dining hall, she sits at the head table. She looks out and waits for me. While the animals eat, she walks out into the courtyard. She looks up at the moon. Soon, cumulus clouds float in and cover it up, and the courtyard grows dark.

Onensis and his fellow cranes land. He signals a few cranes to open the temple gates. The army of golden monkeys marches in. Onensis nods at Annie and says, "We got your message."

She smiles. I look around and am confused. I ask, "How did they all get here? What's going on?"

Annie motions everyone into the dining hall. She stands at the head table and says, "My friends, my family, we've come to prepare for our last and final battle. I need every one of you to believe, not in me, but believe in what is right and what is our destiny. No animal should be a slave to another. Moyen is not our master. The time has come to free ourselves. I'm not here to convince you to fight tomorrow—I know you have all chosen the path ahead. Rather, I want you to all find the clarity of mind to focus. Tonight will be the hardest night of your life. You will hug and cry and long for another time. I know for I've lived it, and I'll live it tonight too. But I will let my hope, my faith triumph over my fears. As the sun rises in the morning and as the swallows perch and sing, dress yourself with determination and slide your sword into your sheath with a sense of purpose. For tomorrow, we will all take back what is ours, the forest, the mountains and the temple."

A loud roar erupts from the crowd. Onensis stands next to Annie. He says, "Cranes and monkeys, we lived here for centuries. This temple is our home. We lost it. Moyen took everything and more. Now, we have to take back what is rightfully ours."

Annie describes the plan to everyone. She breaks the crowd into different groups and tells them what to do. They all listen carefully. She designates several different commanders and meets with them. She asks everyone to rest up before heading out in the morning.

I ask Annie, "What are you going to do?"

"I have to go back now before they find me missing."

"I knew you would figure it out. I knew you wouldn't give up. Be safe."

"I will."

Onensis walks up and says, "Thank you for the message. My answer is: yes, I will not hide."

Annie bows and says, "Good. Where's Rhino?"

"He'll be here soon."

"We need him," she replies.

Onensis bows and thanks Annie. She hands Onensis her shield. She hugs me one more time and then climbs down into her hole.

33. THE WEDDING

Like a centipede across a wet stone, the sun lazily inches its way up the turquoise morning sky, casting its golden rays across the floral meadow. The stone and wood cage thunders down and crashes into the ground. Pika and Red are shaken and dizzy. Moyen laughs. The guards take the two, tie them up and throw them over a horse. Dressed with a crown of red orchids and a yellow floral necklace, Annie sits on a horse behind General Mantchu. Moyen says, "Everyone ride out. Today, we will have peace!"

Moyen and his army march out the two wooden gates. The animals in the palace cheer them as they leave. Annie watches the animals and isn't sure what to think. They genuinely support Moyen and his cause. She wonders, "Can everyone be right from their side?"

The march is slow and methodical. Moyen smiles and awaits his destiny. They approach the camp. He yells, "Open the doors!"

They walk in. The camp is silent. Moyen yells at the guards, "Where are the animals? Wake them up!"

As the guards run towards the huts, they fall into large pits. They scream and howl in pain. Some die as they fall on spears. Some are stuck in the pits and can't get out. The gates swiftly slide shut behind them. At once, Moyen turns to Annie and yells, "What'd you do? Where are they? Bring me Pika and Red!"

The guards look back, and Pika and Red are missing. General Mantchu yells, "Where, where, where? Find them. Imbeciles!"

Moyen signals for everyone to turn around. He grabs Annie with his mouth and hurls her onto the ground. He snarls, "What is this plan? What'd you do?"

Annie crawls toward a boulder and says, "I didn't do anything. I don't know what you're talking about."

Moyen punches her stomach and claws her face. She touches the blood dripping on her face, stands up and says, "Let me go. I don't want to fight."

Moyen lashes out at her again and knocks her down. She hits her head against the boulder and stumbles across the ground. Shaking her head out, she leaps up and bounds off a horse's back. As she hops from horse to horse, she lets out a loud shriek, filling the camp and forest with a sharp cry. She falls to the ground and rolls into a standing position.

Two swords land in her hands. Rhino appears next to her. He hangs her shield on her back. The camp is surrounded by the cranes, monkeys and imprisoned animals. Moyen's army moves back. Some of them fall into pits—dying on the spears or getting stuck in sap. Rhino whispers to Annie, "Pika, Red safe."

She nods and whispers, "Thank you, my friend."

Annie faces Moyen and yells, "Charge!"

Rhino and Annie launch out and fight the soldiers. The cranes and monkeys descend on the army. Moyen's army is entrapped in the camp. Pika and Red sit atop a distant dove tree, watching. They both want to join but realize they're in no condition to fight. Pika sees Annie in the center battling the dholes, tigers and cougars. She adeptly spins and kicks her way around. Like a graceful ballet, she springs, sidesteps and swings the swords to cut and carve up the soldiers. Four to six soldiers always are on the attack of her. She pushes some back while she fights others. She effortlessly switches between her swords and shield. Pika is amazed at his sister. Red also notices and is proud of her pupil, seeing that she listened to everything. Remarkably, Annie's also found her own fighting technique. She uses her long arms and legs to sweep soldiers off their feet and then to leap on them. Red's also proud that Annie's only injuring the soldiers, not killing them. Red would be killing them, but she knows this is a better approach. Pika notices that Annie has to keep wiping the blood from her face. He wonders when the wound will seal.

Pika says, "We should get closer."

"Yes, but it'll be difficult. We aren't strong enough to fight, so we can't get caught. We can't be a distraction to your sister."

"I know."

Pika starts climbing down. Red follows him. They run from tree to tree. They near the camp. They decide not to go in but watch from a large cedar tree that hangs over the fence.

Annie continues to take out Moyen's army. Rhino also does the same. He makes his way and clears out an area. He looks around. Moyen's army is fighting two battles. Annie and Rhino are battling from the inside, and from the outside, the rebels have surrounded and are defeating them slowly but surely. Moyen is on the outskirts fighting the cranes, monkeys, pandas and wolverines. None of them are a challenge for him. Just as Annie and Rhino destroy their enemies, Moyen is easily killing the rebels.

Onensis flies in front of Moyen and says, "Stop Moyen! It's me you want. I was a coward before and asked Leuca to fight my fight. But now, I won't run."

Moyen laughs, "Old bird, do you really think you have a chance?"

He leaps up and takes a giant swipe, knocking Onensis over and breaking his right wing. Onensis lays on the ground. He leaps onto his feet. Moyen approaches, growling. Onensis hurdles over Moyen and digs his claws into Moyen's back before grasping Moyen's tail. Onensis bites Moyen's tail. Moyen lets out a yell and shakes his tail, casting Onensis off. Moyen charges at Onensis and digs his right claws into Onensis's heart. Moyen pulls his hand out and watches Onensis fall to his knees and then collapse. Moyen hurls Onensis' heart away out of disrespect. The other cranes and monkeys see. Some are shocked and distracted, allowing Moyen's soldiers to move in on them.

Moyen says, "Stupid old bird. That was too easy. Another spirit...dead."

Annie and Rhino see Onensis fall. They are more determined. Rhino races towards Moyen. General Mantchu lands in front of him and says, "Hello, hello, hello! Feel good to be traitor?"

"You traitor."

"Nature is kill or be killed. One thing. Why?"

"Confused and hurt. But I know better."

"With this rabbit?" laughs General Mantchu. "They knew truth, they hate you, traitor."

General Mantchu lunges at Rhino with his left wing. His missing right wing doesn't impair him or slow him down. Rhino dodges the attack. He steps aside and pushes General Mantchu past him. He vaults over a log and with his sword slices large pieces of wood shaped like sharp daggers. With his tail, he shoots them at General Mantchu who skillfully evades them. General Mantchu leaps and spins with his tail feathers expanded. The camouflage is blinding. Rhino is lost and tries to find General Mantchu. He can't. General Mantchu slices Rhino's left arm. The pain is sharp, and Rhino drops his sword. He falls down and rolls across the floor. He looks for General Mantchu's feet. He needs to stall, so he starts talking. "Never betrayed. Just made bad choice."

"Bad decision. Follow human," snarls General Mantchu.

"Annie one of us. Fights for us."

"Ha! Human and an ugly rabbit. She don't care. Just want to be human. She'll be gone."

"Wrong," says Rhino, dodging General Mantchu's attacks.

"Lie to yourself. I tell how it is. I don't lie." With his tail, General Mantchu throws a feather knife that cuts the right shoulder of Rhino. He grabs it and sees the blood on his hand.

Rhino says, "Is that all? You're in trouble then."

General Mantchu launches several more feather knives. Two of them are daggers that hit Rhino in the stomach and in the left thigh. He falls to the ground. He can't move very quickly. General Mantchu approaches and asks, "Where is unicorn?"

Rhino looks up at General Mantchu and smiles. General Mantchu punches his right cheek. Rhino collapses. General Mantchu yells, "Tell me!"

Rhino rolls over onto his back. Blood pours out of the corners of his mouth as he smiles. He pulls the daggers out of his stomach and thigh. He screams in pain and struggles to stand. He says, "Learned from Annie. My purpose defines my life. No purpose before. Annie true and sincere. Found mine."

He sees General Mantchu's feet. He uses his tail to sweep him off his feet. "Destroy you."

General Mantchu lets out a yell. He tries to get back to his feet, but Rhino leaps on top of him before he can. Rhino punches his face several times. Rhino takes his other sword and holds it up against General Mantchu's neck. General Mantchu says, "Kill me. Coward."

"Death is easy," Rhino says. He flips General Mantchu over and cuts off his tail and left wing. General Mantchu howls in pain and lays on the ground with the blood pouring out. Rhino takes some wood pieces and pins him to the ground. "Watch this fall."

34. SPRING

Soldiers fall one by one. Soon only a few of Moyen's soldiers remain. Moyen stands near the center of the camp. Annie approaches him. They are surrounded by the cranes, wolverines, pandas and monkeys. Although we significantly outnumber Moyen's army, we know we are fighting a spirit, and the odds can turn quickly. With Onensis dead, we don't know how we'll kill Moyen. Rhino leans on his sword in the back near the huts where he hovers over General Mantchu.

Pika and Red have climbed down and entered the camp, standing behind the rebels. I see them and run over to them. I tell them Onensis was killed. They tell me they saw. We all know that Moyen will be hard to subdue.

Moyen smirks at Annie and says, "You must think it's over and that you've won."

"No, I know better," says Annie.

"Very good, you indeed would've made a good wife. How do you suppose this will end?"

"You let us leave with our freedom. You go into hiding."

"Ha! I do like you. You realize that none of you can kill me. Only another spirit can kill me. I'm the only spirit left, so I'll be the only one left standing. Let's make this simple. Come, be my wife, and we'll forget this all happened."

"Forget it!" yells Annie. She charges at Moyen and kicks him in the face. She leaps, spins and kicks him again. He brushes off the attacks

146

and smirks. He advances towards her, snickering.

Annie grabs her swords and swoops in on his hind legs. Moyen steps to the side and pushes her down. Annie bounces back up, grabs her swords, and flips over towards Moyen. She dives underneath his belly and tries to stab him. The swords break on contact. Moyen falls down, crushing Annie. He stands back up and says, "Oops, I felt a tickle."

Annie rolls over to get away. A piercing pain runs up her spine. She pulls the shield off her back. She can barely stand up. She knows she's hurt. She can't run. A tingling sensation runs up from her toes to her spine, leaving behind it a trail of numbness. Her hands can't hold the broken swords. She tumbles over. She grabs her stomach and sees her blood-soaked hands—her face looks up at Moyen as she realizes she fell on her swords. She's cut and bleeding. She pulls her swords out of her stomach and covers her wounds with her hands. Moyen ambles up to her. He steps on the shield, breaking it into tiny pieces. She doesn't know what to do. She knows she can't fight anymore. Does she agree to marry him and end this? If she doesn't, everyone is doomed. He'll kill them all.

Moyen roars in victory. The camp and forest shake from his voice. Despair cascades throughout the rebels. We don't know what to do. Moyen rolls Annie over and says, "You should've agreed. Now look. You're as good as dead. Your friends are dead. Pika and Red—they're dead."

Annie's eyes close. The sharp, piercing pain in her stomach and up and down her spine are unbearable. Her body is shutting down—her fingers and toes tingle, her ears only pick up the sound of the wind, her tongue is dry, and her heart beats slower and slower. She hears Moyen say 'Pika'. She opens her eyes and tries to find him. She wants to see him one last time. She doesn't see him anywhere near. She yells, "Pika! Pika!"

Moyen places his right paw on her, crushing her back into the swords. The sharp pain in her back is unbearable. Annie screams and writhes in agony. She shrieks. All of us rebels cover our ears and bury our faces. We can't stand to watch. Moyen draws his paw back and slowly snaps out a single claw. He says, "Goodbye Annie."

Moyen drives his claw into Annie. "What?!"

His claw is jammed by two swords. Pika lays on top of Annie with two swords blocking the claw. He uses all his might against Moyen who pushes more and more. The claw inches towards Pika's face. Moyen smiles smugly and says, "What is it that you humans say? Kill two birds with one stone. How appropriate. Now, you two can watch each other die."

As his shoulder reaches back to strike one more time, Moyen neck slumps, and he collapses onto them. His claw remains caught between the swords. His eyes roll back. His mouth is opened and gasps for a breath. The muscles that were strong and virile are slowly sagging and wilting. All his strength quickly vanishes. Pika has no idea what's happening. Pika pushes the claw off of them. Their bodies still are trapped under Moyen's paw and chest. Pika uses his hands and feet to push Moyen off. He rolls Annie over and carries her a few feet away. He removes the sword from her. Pika talks to her, but she doesn't respond. Hearing a slight heartbeat and seeing her chest slightly move with her breath, he feels comforted and lays her down.

Pika looks at Moyen. All of Moyen's soldiers drop their weapons and surrender. The rebels cheer and race in. They take the soldiers captive. They fall silent as they near Pika and Annie. Pika asks Red to watch Annie. Pika walks over to Moyen. He walks around to Moyen's back. He lifts Moyen up slightly. He sees a familiar tail. Pika yells for someone to pull this animal out.

I can't contain it anymore. It's me! Yes, I was the one who killed Moyen! I'm passed out but still clinging to a sword. I had passed out when Moyen landed on me. Pika carries me over to Red. Yes, Osani, I'm not lying. It was me!

"Naso! Naso!" cries Pika.

I slowly open my eyes. I look over at Moyen and grin. I mumble, "I did it."

Pika hugs me and says, "Yes, you did. How?"

"I used Onensis' sword."

Pika keeps hugging me and says, "That was brilliant!"

"How's Annie?"

Pika starts to cry and says, "She's not good."

35. THE RABBIT PRINCESS

"Are you sure you don't want to stay?" asks Red.

"Yes, I'm sure," replies Annie. "I have unfinished business."

"But you're part of our family now. We can help you."

"I know. That's why I know I can leave. I can always come back. And I will."

Red tries to convince her to stay one last time and says, "Didn't you always want to be a ruler again?"

"I did," laughs Annie. "Oh, I did. Pika knows fully well how terribly I wanted to. But in all our pain and suffering, I've learned there's more to life. That's what I want to find."

Red smiles and knows she can't convince Annie to stay. She looks at her with admiration at how she's changed. She never believed someone could change that much.

Our small room in the temple seems smaller with all our close friends inside. Our beds are clean and made, and our bags sit on the bottom of the beds. Red, Rhino and I stand along the back wall. Annie looks out the window and tries to remember everything she sees—the mountains and cliffs, Black Crane Falls, and the morning sunlight falling across the far off valley. She sighs and tries not to cry. She turns around and looks at her brother.

Pika tightens the strings on Annie's backpack made out of thick dove tree leaves. For fun, I had drawn three dragons on it. He secures it against his own bag and puts his arms through the straps. He walks across the room to Red and gives her a hug. Annie limps over to Red and hugs her too. She leans on Pika to hold herself up. Rhino walks over and hugs them.

"Thank you. My hero," says Rhino.

"I'm no hero, Rhino. I'm no hero," blushes Annie. She really is embarrassed by compliments now and prefers to be just a regular kid like everyone else.

Rhino grins and hugs her again.

Red says, "Rhino is right. Thank you. Thank you for everything."

"This isn't goodbye. I don't want to cry. We're family now. We'll see each other again. Take care of yourselves and this temple," says Annie.

"Where going?" asks Rhino.

"I don't know."

"Tell us."

"I really don't know. Ask Pika and Naso. We have no idea."

Pika and I nod our heads. Annie adds, "We'll either go back over the mountains to find some answers. Rather, I want to find some answers. Or we'll go back into the valley and see what remains from our past. I don't know at this point. Please keep everyone safe."

Rhino and Red nod. Annie pats Pika on the shoulder to signal him to leave. Pika says, "Take care friends."

Annie follows Pika out the door, holding onto his shoulder. Their backpacks bounce off his back and push off against her arm. I follow close behind. We walk down the long stone hallway. Feeling the cool morning mountain air against her cheeks, she doesn't remember much from the past few months of recovery. She only knows what the other animals have told her.

Carrying my own little bag, I ask, "Annie, have you decided where we're going yet?"

Annie laughs and says, "I have no idea."

"Why don't we stay another day? What's the rush?"

"I have to start holding my own just like everyone else. I'm sure most animals don't know where they're going. Why do we have to?"

"I just like to know."

"You didn't before," smiles Annie.

We turn the corner and walk into the courtyard. All the animals have gathered to say goodbye. Annie is overcome with emotion. She holds Pika's shoulder tight. He takes her hand in his. The animals cheer her and cry our names. We are showered with flower petals.

The crowd opens a path for us to walk out of the temple. Chills go down my spine. I've never felt so humble or unworthy in my life. We slowly walk down a newly formed trail of crimson and gold flower petals.

Red and Rhino approach from behind and stand on a stage. Red waves her hands to silence the crowd. The crowd quiets down. Annie, Pika and I turn around. Red smiles at us and says to the crowd, "Spirits come to us in different ways. We have known many. Onensis. Leuca. Qilin. Even Moyen. When I first met these three here, I honestly didn't think much of them. I thought these humans would ruin us. And I didn't know what a little mouse was doing with them. I thought they would never understand us. I believed these humans would never be one of us. The Heavens again showed me how silly and wrong I was. Pika, you believed in us and bridged our worlds through your morality, devotion and courage. Naso, you rose above all of us to find the genius and bravery to kill Moyen. Annie, our dear, dear Annie, you are the reason why Qilin came back. You gave us hope in our darkest time."

Red takes a deep breath, holding back her emotions. She stands tall, raises her arms and exults, "Everyone, this is your princess! Your Rabbit Princess!"

Annie blushes and bows her head in appreciation. The crowd surrounds us and cheers. The crowd lifts us up and carries us out the courtyard. We are brought to the entrance of the temple and set down. The three of us stand before the crowd. We all bow and turn around. Annie looks towards her left and sees the giant cliffs with the sun peeking out at the top. She turns to the right and sees the rocky trail back down the mountain with the valley sprawled out below.

"Which way?" asks Pika.

Annie closes her eyes and points that way.

EPILOGUE. THE MOON RISES

Osani, I'm tired. It's time for me to sleep. I'll finish the story later. The sun is so high up. It's way past my bedtime. I'm old. I must sleep. Throughout history, war has always existed. I was hopeful my children and my grandchildren would never have to experience it, but Blue has different plans. I should've told this story to you long ago.

You should rest too. You have a busy night. I'm sure it'll be a clear night when the moon streams across the canyon.

ABOUT THE AUTHOR

R. Chen was born surrounded by the bridges of Portland, Oregon. He grew up playing in the streets and woods, and chasing his imagination through stories and drawings. When the world told him to grow up, he did just that— he got a tie, a watch, a job and a car (not necessarily in that order), and he did well. One day, while holding his two young children, he realized he wasn't done chasing his imagination. And now he's doing just that—teaching his children that one should never stop chasing one's imagination.

Made in the USA
Monee, IL
14 December 2019

18486554R00095